GOING TO THE SPACES

THE INTERPLANETARY OUTSIDE WORLD

ASHWINI D. K

Made with ♥ on the Notion Press Platform
www.notionpress.com

This book is dedicated to my father,

Krishnamurthy E,

with love.

Contents

Preface

This story was born from a question that haunted me:What if time itself could feel pain? The idea stayed with me for years until I finally gave it life in these pages.

Writing this novel was a journey. One that took me through endless drafts, sleepless nights and moments of doubt. But in the end, the characters refused to be silenced.

This is not just a science fiction tale-it's a story of love, destination, survival and the fragile bond between human connection and the outer world extraterrestrial species besides its obstacles.

To those who open this book. I hope you find within these pages something that sparks curiosity, emotion or even just a moment of wonder.

Thank you for stepping into this world with me. Let the story begin.

CHAPTER ONE

AAYUN'S FAMILY

He dreamed once of flying high,
Touching the stars, reaching the sky.
But fate had stitched a simpler thread,
A life of endeavor, a path well-spread.

Yet delight was not in distant beams,
But in the love that shaped his dreams.
With hands that carved, with eyes so bright,
Bharath built small worlds in wood and light.

Beside him stood a soul so wise,
Abhyartha, with joy in her eyes.
A voice of strength, a heart so free,
She saw the world as it should be.

No walls confined their hopes and art,
They shaped with skill, with hand and heart.
Toy by toy, their craft took flight,
Bringing young minds endless light.

Their son would watch, his fingers learn,
As wooden wheels began to turn.
Not riches vast, nor fame untold,
Yet happiness, more pure than gold.

For dreams may shift, yet never die,
They live in hands, in hearts, in sky.
Not all must chase a distant gleam,
Some find their stars within a dream.

One early morning Bharath (Aayun's father) was ploughing the land thinking about his dreams that he did not accomplish his ambitions by just being a common farmer. He finished farming stuff and went back to his home. His wife Abhyartha (Aayun's mother) all she made was a delicious food to her beloved husband.

He came, Honey! Said Abhyartha to Bharath.
Why you are not okay in these days? Said Abhyartha.
No, I'm okay, said Bharath.
'Always thinking about the past, but not living in a present breathe,' said Abhyartha.
Do you know dear, said Bharath: "Life is all about living, money, fame and all, but once you have thought about your past, it is full of turmoils that breaks us like a nuclear fission?"It's okay honey, life is not about fame, money and all. It's about, whether you are poor or elite,

happiness is the ultimate in irrespective of the positive or negative vibes. And you should be happy with your work that you do and you must have a sensory within you okay, said Abhyartha

Yeah, I do accept that whatever you're saying, said Bharath.

Happiness and peace within inner self is the ultimate, said Abhyartha.

Okay dear, let's have dinner together, said Bharath.

The dawn and dusks were going well. One day he realized that he should lead a happy and peaceful life by breaking his turmoil's.

As usual he was going to agricultural market to sell his produce. While he was coming back on the way to his house, Charavana (Bharath's neighbor) asked him that 'Why don't you guys have kids? It's been five years that you have been combed your family.'

Yeah, She is facing some Gynic issue, everything of her gynic crisis would be resolved after some couple of days, said Bharath.

That's great, said Charavana.

Bharath back to his home and said, dear, 'If we'll gonna be parents or not in the coming future, it doesn't matter for me.' It's a nonsense. I do take care and love you, that's all I wanted with peace.

Anyway we'll try out hospital, that's the last one, said Abhyartha.

Okay then, said Bharath.

Over a period of time, her problem got resolved and she is conceived.

Hurrah! Today I'm the ultimate blissful guy in this world, said Bharath.

Wait! 'She might not gonna conceive in near future, this might be the last one,' said Ayura (Doctor).

What do you mean doctor? Said Bharath.

I mean, this would be the last foetus. Take care of it, said Ayura.

That's okay. Fine. Atleast we would be happy in these period of gestation. Each and every day of her gestation period brings us more twinkling stars in our life, said Bharath.

That's the life you man, said Ayura.

On Friday evening, Abhyartha could able to feel the pre-delivery pain and the baby boy is born.

'His face is like a pinkish petals of rose and he just came out of his mother's womb to fill the gloomy skies into our heart,' said Bharath.

Now the responsibility of this kid has began. "He might be the last one or he may not be the last one," said Abhyartha.

It's okay, we'll put our efforts to make him a better version of himself, said Bharath.

In our country, our people will do naming ceremony for a kid in family. But, I'm not interested in this stuff, we'll just name him, there is no necessity to make it as a big deal, said Bharath.

We'll save these coins to his future or to fulfill his dreams, said Abhyartha.

You are a god gift to us and you should contribute greatest gift to the world. So we are naming you as Aayun.

One morning, Bharath had talk about his dreams to his beloved wife, 'I was dreamt to become an astronaut, but everything has been changed due to my family issues, so I ended up being farmer.'

Ahhh... I'm okay with whatever you're having today, said Abhyartha.

Now it's the turn of Bharath to do his farming activities. 'His ploughing skills as if like a warrior, who born to fight against his rivalry to kill out pests and diseases and breaking the compact soil just like breaking ice on a frozen pond.'

Bharath, is this necessary to spread polythene sheets on soil? Said Abhyartha.

Yep, it do conserves soil moisture, it do escapes from diseases and no weeds at all. It can reduce drudgery, said Bharath.

What crop do you wanna grow this time? Said Abhyartha.

We'll grow strawberry, said Bharath.

How do you cultivate strawberry? Said Abhyartha.

Through 'RUNNERS' said Bharath.

What do you mean by that? Said Abhyartha.

It's a propagating material to produce strawberry, said Bharath.

Why do you want only this fruit crop? Said Abhyartha.

Because, it's bit like a commercial fruit crop, so that income would be more. And in turn it would be helpful to raise our child, said Bharath.

Then, I do help through your farming journey, said Abhyartha.

Ohh! Women in agriculture, hahaha... said Bharath.

Then I'm so excited to do planting like a queen, said Abhyartha.

Then, I do take care of enemies like pests and diseases in this way, said Bharath. Hey, I forgot to ask you one thing by the way, what about irrigation? Said Abhyartha.

Through 'Drip irrigation' means it do consists of mains, submains, laterals and emitters just as a pipe system my dear wife and we do follow this method, mainly because it is more efficient in terms of water use, said Bharath.

Ohh, that's great! Said Abhyartha.

'We did planting like as if we reached sea voyage and we're spreaded a polythene sheets like a royal carpet,' said Abhyartha.

Taking care of plants, seems to be like neonatal care, said Bharath.

Yeah, obviously, said Abhyartha.

Honey, said Abhyartha.

Yes dear, what will happen after this? I mean after planting, said Abhyartha.

There is a term called 'flowering' do occurs in this process, then after that fertilization do happens and after that fruit setting. We can see these development one after the other, said Bharath.

Okay, moving on, irrigation management is the most important thing, said Bharath.

Exactly, said Abhyartha.

Okay then. Hurry up dear, said Bharath.

It's ringing... It's ringing...It's just a knocking sound of our home. In this dusky time who has come, see who they are, said Abhyartha.

Okay then, I will see, door was opened by Bharath, it's a surprise for them. It's their in-laws. Ohh, father-in-law and mother-in-law welcome home. We are seeing you after so long.

Yeah, actually we came to see our grandchild, said in-laws of Bharath.

Mom and dad I'm happy to see you here, said Abhyartha. Just right now, I've prepared the food, let's have it.

First we would like to see our grand kid, said in-laws.

Yeah sure, come we'll see him, said Bharath.

Ohh, little cuteepie, it's you, we are happy for you, said in-laws.

Obviously, the kid won't talk, only he could do burb, make some noises and fed out by his mother.

Why can't you have another child? Said Abhyartha's mother.

Mom why do you want another child? Said Abhyartha.

Because, just to accompany him. You will also be happy and family would get completed, said Abhyartha's mother.

That's pretty cool mom, said Abhyartha.

Then what about the couple having no kids after getting married. What would be their situation? Said Bharath.

Why? What's the matter, what happened to you my dear son-in-law, said Abhyartha's mother.

No mother-in-law, nothing, said Bharath.

Tell me exactly!

She has faced some gynic problem in her womb, so let her be, said Bharath.

What do you mean! Said Abhyartha's mother.

Yes, she had gone through her gynic treatment, just to overcome her issue, said Bharath.

Ohh, is it so, I can understand being a women, said Abhyartha's mother.

Thank god you have understood, said Bharath.

Why you're saying thanks? Said Abhyartha's mother.

Why because, in our society women is like a material for them, for few 'she is like a thorn on the clothes and also like a fire on the womb.' She do care of her family, parents, in-laws and home. She will do chore work, she do care about children and all she will do is sacrifice. The one that is lagging behind is, her career and time just to take care of the family. But one should support her by not discriminating that 'she is meant only for household stuff.'

Men and women should do these chores equally, then woman can empower in each and everyfield. And sometimes, she do sacrifice also. When it comes to her health, at foremost she do face her menstrual cycle starting at the age of 12-15 years, it's not the thing that I'm saying, but it's like a taboo in some places, when she attains her puberty. It's just a waste in the form of unfertilized eggs coming out from her uterus due to harmonal changes. Can't we say it's just a common and natural process. It's just a common science in our livelihood and she has to face this Dysmenorrhea till menopause or it may extend also in one or the other consequences.

When it comes to her motherhood, if she fulfills her famiy needs, I mean if she carries zygote, it's fine for them. Suppose if she does'nt means, I mean due to involuntary infertility, they do blame her. After that, she might become empty nester, in her age old days, may be sooner or later also sometimes. The best thing in this world she'll do is crèche care. During her delivery, she has to face the pelvic pain that occurs, it's all about her do or die situation. Even after her delivery also, she might be facing some pelvic inflammatory diseases as well. Then after that family stuff do comes here and she could able to handle household chores. In a typical family sometimes, they are more curious to know about women's family issue. And here how it goes like this, Is she got married? Is she fine there? Is she divorced? She is living life without her husband. She is a single parent. These are all the issues that only my wife or every women of this world are facing today, said Bharath.We are very proud of you! Said Abhyartha's parents.

It's not about knowing the stuff, it's about understanding, said Bharath.
Yep son-in-law, you are right , said his in-laws.
Men and women should equally give her right to take her health of her choice in a right way, said Bharath.
Yeah, we do accept, said his in-laws. Ohh, okay. Okay feminist, come on let's have dinner together, said Abhyartha. Okay, come on then, move on, said Bharath. Wow! It is scrumptious, said Abhyartha's parents. Thank you mom and dad said Abhyartha.

Had food, okay guys have a restful sleep, said Abhyartha's parents. Okay then, said the coulple. On firstlight, okay guys, do take care of yourself and the kid. Will take our leave now, said Abhyartha's parents. Okay, you too take care of your health. Bye. Bye, said Bharath and Abhyartha.
Honey, let's get ready for the field, said Abhyartha.
Okay dear, will move, said Bharath. Switch on the irrigation system, said Bharath.
Okay honey, said Abhyartha.
Ohh my God! See these flowers 'like a milky white clouds, where in the sun is blossoming like a honeydew,' said Abhyartha.
Okay, let's go now, said Bharath.

Come on, said Abhyartha.

One month after that, we should harvest the fruits, said Bharath.

Yeah, will do it, said Abhyartha.

See here, Aayun is whimpering, said Abhyartha.

Ohh, that's cute, said Bharath.

'His cooing is like a pearl in the ocean, we're opening the nacre to see it for the first time,' said Bharath.

Exactly, said Abhyartha.

He is just two months old right now and you should show him to the glow during earlymorning, said Bharath.

Yeah, you are right, he has to get some vital compounds and need to feed him the maternal milk for another five to six months, said Abhyartha.

Hmm... Good, said Bharath.

Dear, do you know one thing? Tomorrow I'm buying 'Ecomac' said Bharath.

What do you mean by that? Said Abhyartha.

It's a wooden bike, said Bharath.

Ohh, that's amazing, said Abhyartha.

Do you know it's features? Said Bharath.

Go on, said Abhyartha.

It do consists of wooden coatings all over the body as a frame and the engine is made up of some metals just to pass out the fuel and they have used physic nut as a biofuel, said Bharath.

And don't you think it will gonna reduce land dumpings to some extent. And then you go for it, said Abhyartha.

Surprise! Take a look over here, said Bharath.

Wow! It's astonishing, the bike that you have been brought here, said Abhyartha.

Come let's have a ride, said Bharath. Ohh, go for it, said Abhyartha.

'In the middle of the zephyr, going like a dragonfly to see the panorama.'

Thank you, said Abhyartha.

I'm deeply obliged, said Bharath.

Come here, we'll go to strawberry field today, said Bharath.

Ha... sure, said Abhyartha.

See here, these fruits, said Bharath.

Wow! It's like an elysium on the earth. Hope we shall see surplus production, said Abhyartha.

Hope so, said Bharath.

Dear, see here, it's time for harvesting, said Bharath.

Okay, we shall do it, said Abhyartha.

Whatever the fruits appears to be pinkish red in color, you just pluck it off, said Bharath.

Okay, my dear husband, said Abhyartha.

Then, after getting over by fewdays, once the fruits transformed from accent color to pinkish red color, we do harvest it afterwards, said Bharath.

Okay, said Abhyartha.

I think we are done with harvesting today, said Bharath.

Hmm... said Abhyartha.

I will head towards market now, vehicle is coming right

now, you move to home and do take care of our kid, said Bharath.

Okay, then I will leave, said Abhyartha.

Sir, shall we go now? Said Meghasta (the driver).

Yeah, said Bharath.

I think you have got nice yield, isn't it? Said Meghasta.

Yes, said Bharath.

I think we have arrived the marketing centre sir, said Meghasta.

Yep, said Bharath.

See there, something is going on this marketing place, said Meghasta.

It seems like a farmer engaging in a heated argument, said Bharath.

Yeah, said Meghasta.

Sir, why you are quarreling here? Said Bharath to the farmer who has engaged in an argument. Because, this time market price is been very low, not even providing the minimum price and this won't even fetch my input costs means whatever the expenses that I have spent on the produce, said the farmer.

So, what you will do? Said Bharath.

What to do, I will sell it and go, said the farmer.

Okay, said Bharath.

I won't sell these produce, we'll go back, said Bharath.

Okay, we'll go sir, said Meghasta.

Thanks for coming sir, said Bharath.

Sir don't be disheartened, said Meghasta.

It's okay, kindly take your driving charge, said Bharath.

Okay, take care sir. Bye said Meghasta.

Okay, Bye. Bye, said Bharath.

Knocking... dear, said Bharath.

Honey, you came up with empty hands, why you didn't sold it? Said Abhyartha.

It's pathetic! Marketing price was very poor there. So I came out from there, said Bharath.

Thats okay. No issue, said Abhyartha.

Hmm... said Bharath.

See here, my dear little one, strawberries here, said Bharath.

Yeah, he is watching out, said Abhyartha.

These strawberries are just glowing like you, said Bharath.

Honey, you don't worry, I have an alternative idea, said Abhyartha.

What ideas do you have? Said Bharath.

I'm good at culinary and baking, I will make some stuff out of this. We'll convert these produce into product and thereby we can earn some money, said Abhyartha.

Wow! That's a nice idea that you have said and this is called women empowerment, said Bharath.

Hahaha... said Abhyartha.

So, tomorrow let's make some advertisement and this is for temporary until strawberries got over, said Bharath.

Hmm... okay, said Abhyartha. So what do you will gonna prepare? Asked Bharath.

I'll gonna prepare: Strawberry candy, strawberry milkshake, strawberry tart and desserts like strawberry cake, said Abhyartha.

Ohh, that's good, said Bharath.

Then I'll gonna make you a Bricked oven to prepare cake and tart said Bharath.

Yep, that's fine, said Abhyartha.

How do you prepare strawberry candy? Said Bharath.

First, do wash strawberries properly, then make a sugar syrup. Then do scroll on the hot sugar syrup. After that dip it in a cold water and it gets crystaised. Finally its ready to serve, said Abhyartha.

Hmm... it's pretty cool! Said Bharath.

Do you want me to prepare anything apart from this? Said Abhyartha. No, that's enough, said Bharath.

Along with you, I will also make some smoothies, said Bharath.

Which one? Asked Abhyartha.

Strawberry milkshake, said Bharath.

Then how do you make this one? Said Abhyartha.I do grind these strawberries using traditional crusher, then on to this juicy sap, I will gonna add soaked sabja seeds. Then after that I do prepare cream using sugar, milk, butter, almonds, then I put it this cream on to the strawberry juice and then finally garnish with the strawberries, said Bharath.

Hmm... that's good, said Abhyartha.

Tomorrow, he is turning six months old, said Bharath.

Ohh, that's great and we should go to hospital for his immunization, said Abhyartha.

Okay dear, we'll head towards that, said Bharath.

'Ohh my dear kid, it's just a small pain when you will get a shot, but it makes you a conquerer by defeating all diseases, so just feel the pain for few seconds,' said Bharath.

Ohh, you have just became a poet now. Hahaha... said Abhyartha.

Honey, let's get ready for hospital, said Abhyartha.

Okay, said Bharath.

Hurrah! You are a warrior now, said Bharath to Aayun.

Dear, tomorrow we'll go to beach, said Bharath.

For what? Asked Abhyartha.

It's a suspence, said Bharath.

Okay, said Abhyartha.

Hurry up, we are getting late, said Bharath.

I'm coming, said Abhyartha.

Hmm... and finally we are here today, said Bharath.

Hi Meghasta, have you brought all the stuff that I have told? Said Bharath.

Yeah, said Meghasta.

Thank you, said Bharath.

It's okay, said Meghasta.

So let's unload the stuff that you have brought, said Bharath.

Okay, said Meghasta.

Okay, thanks for coming, said Bharath.

See here, these are all wooden dustbins, treated with ecofriendly coatings to resist moisture and UV damage and enclosed with lid to protect from animals or wind along with open slat design for airflow and it is color coded as recyclables, organic and non-recyclable waste and consists of removable inner lines made of jute and banana leaves for easy waste collection, said Bharath.

Wow! It is ecofriendly, said Abhyartha.

Let's install, whatever we are doing it today, it's just a part of ecowork, said Bharath.

Hmm... said Abhyartha.

'Ohh my dearest earth, consider me and my wife as a tiny sand grain, which is deposited in the basket of this ocean all along its periphery,' said Bharath.

I think we are done with this work today, said Bharath.

Ha... said Abhyartha.

Shall we go home now? Said Bharath.

Yeah, said Abhyartha.

Honey, what are you doing? Said Abhyartha.

Yes dear, today we are doing water table conservation in our home, will you help me out with this? Said Bharath.

Yeah sure said Abhyartha.

Yesterday, I dug a pit here, said Bharath.

So, what do you want me to do, said Abhyartha.

Here you put one layer of sand using concrete pan or mortar pan and then I do add a layer of stones or pebbles, will keep on doing this until this pit gets filled, said

Bharath.

Hmm... said Abhyartha.

So what does this makes? Said Abhyartha.

When precipitation do occurs, the water infiltrates into this layer and thereby it improves water table and it's a good idea to each and every household, said Bharath.

Wow! It's a good perception, said Abhyartha.

Now, I have to prepare food for Aayun, said Abhyartha.

What do you wanna prepare for him? I do prepare a food using apple and plum: I do boil these fruits using steam and then smash it together, then I will feed him, that's it, said Abhyartha.

Hmm... good, said Bharath.

Aayun see here, your food is ready my child, I will feed you now, eat well, said Abhyartha.

'On this starry sky, every twinkling stars are approaching to feel your glow and shine.'

Dear, good morning... said Bharath. I will go to field and prepare the land, said Bharath.

Hmm... said Abhyartha.

'Sun is watching you to the journey of perspiration, while you are ploughing and then it turns efforts in this land and downpour in the form of rain.'

Bharath, come let's have dinner, said Abhyartha.

Yeah sure, said Bharath.

Tomorrow I want to do puddling for paddy, said Bharath.

This time are we cultivating paddy? said Abhyartha.

Yeah, said Bharath.

This time we'll grow it in a different way said Bharath.

First, I will do puddling along with green leaf manure and green manuring, said Bharath.

Okay, first we'll finish with this, said Abhyartha.

Yeah, said Bharath.

Let's go honey, said Abhyartha.

Will go now, said Bharath.

I will do puddling now, until it get creates an impervious layer, said Bharath.

Dear, add gliricidia and compost, said Bharath.

Okay, said Abhyartha.

I think we are done with this today. You go home, I will prepare seed bed and I will be back okay, said Bharath.

Okay take care, I'll take my leave, said Abhyartha.

Honey, see here, he is crawling, said Abhyartha.

Ohh, it's his first move, said Bharath.

Ha... said Abhyartha.

Dear, tomorrow I'm heading towards some place to buy bamboo poles, said Bharath.

Okay, said Abhyartha.

Dear, I'm back, I brought all the stuff, said Bharath.

Hmm... that's fine, said Abhyartha.

Honey, come on we'll go to field now, said Abhyartha.

Okay then come on, said Bharath.

You just stay here and have some rest over here, said Bharath.

Okay said Abhyartha.

I will do splits out of bamboo poles and I do make some holes on the splitted bamboo surface, said Bharath.

Okay, said Abhyartha.

It's all ready to install now, said Bharath.

Yeah, said Abhyartha.

First of all, I will put some large stones on each corner of the field. Then, I will arrange these bamboo splits all along its periphery, in between these stones exactly at 30 cm apart. I will arrange these splits parallelly, so that it ensures uniform spreading of water, said Bharath.

Ohh, that's cool said, said Abhyartha.

Dear, now I will dig a pit all along the periphery of paddy field, said Bharath.

For what purpose? Said, Abhyartha.

For aquaculture, I mean, I will put some fishes here, so that we'll gonna earn extra money, said Bharath.

That's a nice concept, said Abhyartha.

Wait, you didn't finished about the pit, said Abhyartha.

Yeah, I forgot, let me explain you now, said Bharath.

Go ahead, said Abhyartha.

I will arrange some stone slabs all along the border of the field in a rectangular shape. Then, I will let excess water that is coming out of the irrigation system and then I will put a fish brood, said Bharath.

Hmm... nice, said Abhyartha.

Shall we go home now? Said Bharath.

Okay, said Abhyartha.

I did visited the field today, germination is pretty good

and the seedlings are ready to transplant, said Bharath.

Good... then we should go and finish the work, said Abhyartha.

Okay then, said Bharath.

Shall we start transplanting now, said Abhyartha.

Sure madam, said Bharath.

Ohh, this wetland sucking my legs, said Abhyartha.

Hahaha... said Bharath. Just pull your legs and try to walk and don't stuck on in one place, said Bharath.

Okay, said Abhyartha.

Our work got finished today, shall we go now, said Bharath.

Yeah, said Abhyartha.

Dear, right now I'm heading towards paddy field just to weed out and do care about Aayun, said Bharath.

Hmm... said Abhyartha.

Tadaa... It's time for harvesting, said Bharath.

Wow! Glorious, said Abhyartha.

Dear, I'm heading towards market in order to sell produce, said Bharath.

Okay, said Abhyartha.

See Bharath, our kid has turned one year old, said Abhyartha.

Try saying Appa (father) Aayun.

Paa... said Aayun.

Then you should say Amma (mother), try out my child, said Abhyartha.

Maa... said Aayun.

Today, I will gonna make some toys for him, said Bharath. Then go ahead, what do you wanna make for him? Said Abhyartha.

The bamboo rabbit and the scrolling vehicle using wood, said Bharath.

I'm very curious to know about that and how do you gonna make scrolling vehicle? Said Abhyartha.

Come and see here, I'll gonna show you now, said Bharath.

See here, I have prepared two circle shaped wheels using wood, in between these two I'm gonna join these pillar like material and it is fixed all along its periphery, then after that, in the part of wooden stuff, I had removed some of the portion just to sit him. I made a jute like seat belt in its middle part of it and I have fixed two wheels, along with I made a large wheel in between these two wheels. Here on this floor, I've prepared single row like a rail bridge in square shape and you can fix a hook for that and play like aerial tramway inside the house, said Bharath.

That's impressive! Said Abhyartha.

Aayun come here, do play with your toys, said Abhyartha.

Yes mom, said Aayun.

Now he could able to speak and play, said Bharath.

Haa... said Abhyartha.

Dear, tomorrow I'm heading towards forest and I'll teach him about forest species, said Bharath.

That's a nice thing that you're doing, said Abhyartha.

Aayun, this is being your first travel to connect with the nature, see Aayun these are all trees, said Bharath.

Ohh nice, said Aayun.

I will gonna teach you one by one, said Bharath. This one is Teak... Sandal...Sisso...Rain tree...Bamboo...

It's very interesting stuff Appa said, Aayun.

Will go back now, said Bharath.

Okay, said Aayun.

What are you staring at? Aayun.

Mom, over there that bubble wands. It's nice actually, said Aayun.

Do you want that? Said Abhyartha.

Yep mom, said Aayun.

But, I won't allow him to play with that stuff, I have other alternative, said Bharath.

What's that? Said Abhyartha.

Jatropha, said Bharath.

What you will gonna do with that? Said Abhyartha.

Just wait, Aayun come here, said Bharath.

Aayun this is called Jatropha. This leaf is attached to the stick like petiole, just leave 2 to 3 cm of petiole and then partially pluck it off, then after you do find a petiole layer, then slide it down to the bottom of the leaf, where in petiole attached to the leaf and then you find a bubble layer over there and then just blow it, said Bharath.

Wow! It's a magic stuff, said Aayun.

Its natural bubble wands. Hahaha... said Bharath.

Guys come on, let's have dinner together, said Bharath.

Okay, said Aayun.

Aayun, there will be a surprise tomorrow, said Bharath.

I'll be waiting Appa, said Aayun.

See here Aayun, these are all letters from A to Z, I prepared using natural rubber. You should learn one by one.

Here, this one is A... and this one is Z... said Bharath.

Appa A... B...C......Z said Aayun.

Okay, keep it up, said Bharath.

Amma, tomorrow I'll go with Appa to visit farm field, said Aayun.

For what? Said Abhyartha.

Just for a walk, said Aayun.

Okay, said Abhyartha.

Appa, this farming field is wonderful! Said Aayun.

What do you wanna become in future? Said Bharath. I will be a farmer like you, but I do grow a crops in the sky, said Aayun.

Gosh! How do you go there? Said Bharath.

I will gonna fly and get there, said Aayun.

Okay, I'll support you, said Bharath.

Aayun, whats in your hand? Said Aabhyartha.

Amma, these are newborn rats, said Aayun.

What! Said Aabhyartha.

Pamper these Amma, their mom left these cuties. That's why I brought here, said Aayun.

Have you seen her mom? Said Aabhyartha.

No, Amma, said Aayun.

Bharath, go and leave them back to their place.

And you Aayun go along with your Appa, said Aabhyartha.

Okay, said Bharath.

Dear, me and Aayun we are going to each and every home to plant a saplings in our native, said Bharath.

Okay, have a nice day, said Aabhyartha.

Appa, whats these for? Said Aayun.

This is to create an awareness regarding plant diversity in order to safegaurd environment, said Bharath.

Ohh, that's good, said Aayun.

Okay, let's go now, said Bharath.

Okay Appa, said Aayun.

Tomorrow, I will gonna clean lake along with that, I do plant pollutant absorbing plants like lily and vetiver grass, said Bharath.

That's a nice initiative, said Aabhyartha.

Come on guys, let's have dinner, said Bharath.

Yeah, come on then, said Aayun.

Tomorrow, there is Aayun's admission for school, said Bharath.

Wow! Said Aabhyartha.

Aayun, today it's your time for admission, get ready okay, said Bharath

Okay Appa, said Aayun.

Hello teacher, I'm seeking admission to my child Aayun for grade one in your little kids school. As I believe it offers excellent academic and extracurricular opportunities, said Bharath.

Yeah that's for sure, said the teacher.

Okay thank you, I will take my leave now. Aayun study well, enjoy your class and I will pick you up by evening, said Bharath.

Appa I'm afraid of school, said Aayun.

Don't worry my son, everything will be okay, make friends and have fun said Bharath.

Hmm... okay Appa. That's my child, careful okay. Bye, said Bharath.

Aayun, how was your school today? Said Abhyartha.

Yeah, it went well, said Aayun.

That's good, said Bharath.

What your teachers have taught today? Said Bharath.

They taught respect for elders, said Aayun.

Hmm... good, said Abhyatha.

Students, today you should do plant and watering to the tiny plants over here, our motive is to conserve the forest okay, come let's one by one do plant and watering, said the school teachers.

Then after that you can disperse okay, said the school principal.

Ohh my dear cute little one, why you are here? We'll go to home after watering okay, come I will pick you to the home and I will introduce you to my parents, said Aayun.

Appa and Amma I'm here, said Aayun.

Give me your bag, said Bharath.

Okay take it Appa, you will be surprised today, said Aayun.

Ohh, what's the matter? I will open it for you now. Aahh! It's a snake, why did you brought it here? It's dangerous. Can't you come with an empty hand, said Bharath. Thank God it's not poisonous, said Abhyartha.

Next time you should be careful okay, said Bharath.

You should not pick like this okay, said Abhyartha.

He is not aware of these species. I think he has mesmerized with the snake colour, said Abhyartha.

Yeah, next time be cautious okay, said Bharath.

Okay Appa, said Aayun.

Appa, today our teachers handled equality classes to us, said Aayun.

Ohh, that's great, said Bharath.

Appa tomorrow we are going to excursion for science and historical museum said Aayun.

Ohh that's nice, Bharath.

Aayun, what you have seen today? Said Bharath.

We saw some planets like Venus and Mars through telescope in science museum said, Aayun.

Good, said Bharath.

Amma, Bye. Bye. I am going to school right now, said, Aayun.

Appa do you know, what did I learnt today. Today some doctors came to our school and they taught us,how to make first aid, said Aayun.

That's good, said Abhyartha

And also, we went to some slums there we learnt about the ethics class about understanding someone's situations on their behalf, said Aayun.

Appa today our teachers have given some homework like sweeping and I need to arrange improper things in our home with video I suppose to send it to the school, said Aayun.

It's a nice activity in school. So that kids could learn their basic activities as early as possible and it creates awareness about hygiene as well.

Okay then I will make a video, said Bharath.

Okay Appa, said Aayun.

Students see here, today it's a sowing class related to agriculture, the thing you need to study basic concept about watering and sowing, said the teachers.

Sowing seeds on portrays seems to be very easy, said Aayun.

Good job students, now you can disperse, said the teachers.

A boy once walked a lonely way,
Beneath the sky so dim and gray.
And there he found, in silent plea,
A wounded soul beneath a tree.

Its breath was weak, its eyes were low,
A fragile heart that faded to glow.
With hands so soft, with voice so light,
He whispered, "You will be alright."

He wrapped it warm, he healed with care,
With love so deep, so pure, so rare.
Not just with herbs, nor thread, nor tie,
But with his kindness, soft and high.

And as it healed, so bright, so free,
They roamed the fields, the sky, the sea.
Not books alone their minds had fed,
But tales the swaying skies said.

The stars became their lantern bright,
The river sang them songs at night.
They studied earth, they studied sky,
Through touch, through sight, through heart, through eye.

For some may learn from ink and scroll,
But wisdom breathes in love's own soul.
And knowledge, pure, and deep, and true,
Lies in the hearts that care for you.

On the way to home, ohh my God! What happened to
you? Let's go to home now, said Aayun.
Appa, see here he is bleeding, said Aayun.

What happened to him? Said Abhyartha.

It's a monkey that is bleeding, said Bharath.

Actually when I was on the way to home, this monkey was squealing and bleeding, said Aayun.

Okay let's hurry up, give it to me, I will go to animal care hospital, said Bharath.

Okay Appa, said Aayun.

Are you okay now? Is it hurting, said Aayun.

He can't speak, said Abhyartha.

Doctor suggested to come over there for regular checkups until he gets healed, said Bharath.

Aayun, you have saved one life today, keep it up my boy, said Abhyartha.

Appa, I wanna name, him said Aayun.

Yeah sure, you can name him, said the couple.

'APRICON' I want to name him as Apricon (The monkey).

Now are you okay Apricon? Said Apricon.

Yeah, he seems to be okay now, said Bharath

Shall we leave him to the forest, said Abhyartha.

No! Let him take a rest. I won't leave him, said Aayun.

Aayun that's not fair, how long will you keep him here. Let him join their family, said Bharath.

For few more days I will keep him, said Abhyartha.

Abhyartha make some food to Apricon. I'll gonna feed him, said Bharath.

Okay then, said Abhyartha.

Today it's saturday, I use to like that dance in our school. No it's like an exercise along with a dance using basketball and that seems to be pretty cool, said Aayun.

Okay enjoy, said Abhyartha.

Students do some innovative exhibition, whoever will do the best, they will gonna get a price, said the teacher.

Okay sir, said the students.

Appa, I'll gonna do Eco bridge along with the thermal sensors.

How do you make that one? Said Bharath.

I do make a dual paths, one for the wildlife and another for the humans wherever hilly Terrains are there. For humans I do install solar panels like in a replaceable manner, if people do walk on that, power generation do happens. By using this power, I do install thermal sensors, it will screen out the robbers who ever comes to threaten or try to rob the animals in forest. The signals will gonna send the information to the forest department, said Aayun.

It's a good idea, said Bharath.

Amma, I got a first prize, said Aayun.

Congratulations, said Abhyartha.

Hey, Apricon. How are you holding up? Said Aayun.

Say hello, have a try, said Aayun.

Hello, Said Apricon.

Wow! He just talked, it's amazing, said Aayun.

Appa, he is talking actually, said Aayun.

He is a special one, said the couple.

We'll leave him to the forest, said the couple.

No Appa, said Aayun.

Apricon, do you wanna go to your place? Said Aayun.

No Appa, he is making 'girneys.' I think he won't go it seems, leave him, said Aayun.

Okay, whenever he wants to go we'll allow him to go, until then he will be fine here, said the couple.

Then it's fine, said Aayun.

Aayun, tomorrow we are all going to visit wetlands, said Bharath.

For what purpose we are going up there? Said Aayun.

For recreational purpose and to see some indigenous varieties of paddy there, said Bharath.

Okay, that's quite interesting, said Aayun.

See here, this one is Kalajeera rice usually cultivate in Koraput, Odisha. I brought it from there. It appears to be black during harvesting time, but at the time of milling appears to be white, said Bharath.

Wow! It's nice, said Aayun.

Apricon, what you are doing? Said Aayun.

I'm typing using your keyboard, said Apricon.

I will be teaching you alphabets okay. Do you want to learn? Said Aayun.

Yeah sure, said Apricon.

I will type for you now. This is called A and I will teach you how to write also, is it okay for you? Said Aayun.

Yep, said Apricon.

Day by day you should learn like this, keep it up my boy,

said Aayun.

Apricorn, what are you doing? Aayun doesn't have head louse, said Abhyartha. Hahaha... said Aayun.

Amma, I will take him to the school, said Aayun.

Is that the school staff will gonna allow him? Said Abhyartha.

He could able to manage few things like he can talk and he is learning alphabets, said Aayun.

It's left to you. Let them give a permission to you first, said Aayun.

I will gonna convince them Amma, said Aayun.

Okay, said Abhyartha.

Appa, come with me, I wanna buy a clothes and bag for Apricon, said Aayun.

Okay come with me. Amma explained everything to me, said Bharath

Hello teacher, said Aayun.

What's this? A monkey with a cloth and bag, said the teacher.

This is my father's second son, said Aayun.

What's wrong with you Aayun, said the teacher.

Sir, I'm sorry. Let me explain you now. His name is Apricon, he can't live without me. I'm pampering him since it was a 'mormoset.' I beg you, even I can't live without him as well, said Aayun.

Then what you want me to do now, said the teacher.

Sir, my father will bear his fee, just he will come with me and he do study here. He won't bother anyone in the class. I will assure you that, said Aayun.

Okay, I believe in you, said the teacher.

Thank you teacher, said Aayun.

Okay, come to the class now, said the teacher.

Okay sir, said Aayun.

Student's this is Apricon, he is Aayun's brother, said the teacher.

Hahaha... said the students.

Don't laugh at him, he will study here. Be cooperative with him, don't make fun out of Apricon. Did you understand, what I'm saying, said the teacher.

Yes teacher, said the students.

He won't bother you as well okay, said the teacher.

Okay teacher, said the students.

Students, now it's a mathematics class using abacus. It's an age old tradition okay, said the teacher.

Okay teacher, said the students.

How was the class today? Said the couple.

It went good, said Aayun.

What your teachers told to you about Apricon? Said the couple.

I convinced them Amma, said Aayun.

Apricon's learning skills are improving day by day, said Bharath.

Yes Appa, said Aayun.

Okay, everybody come here, let's have dinner, said Bharath.

Okay Appa, said Aayun.

From tomorrow onwards we will be having summer holidays. I will gonna enjoy with Apricon, said Aayun.

Okay guys, said Bharath.

I will gonna teach you some skills okay, said Aayun.

Okay, said Apricon.

Apricon, come here, see this window, open this up and close it down, said Aayun.

Okay, I will do it for you, it's very easy, said Apricon.

That's my boy, said Aayun.

Let me teach you some fruits and vegetables name okay, said Aayun.

This one is tomato, say along with me, said Aayun.

Here, this one is apple said Aayun.

This one is apple, said Apricon.

You are a good learner Apricon, said Aayun.

Apricon we'll go to farm now and show me how you will gonna pluck flowers and the fruits said Aayun.

Okay then, come on, let's go, said Apricon.

And here it goes like this and I did it, said Apricon.

Keep it up Apricon, said Aayun.

Let's go home now, said Aayun.

Okay, said Apricon.

Apricon come let's have shower.

Ohh, do you even know how to do shower also said Aayun. Yeah, I know said Apricon.

Amma what you have been prepared today? Said Aayun.

Wanna prepare now, said Abhyartha.

Amma, I will also try said Apricon.

Yeah sure, said Abhyartha.

I will gonna prepare rice said Apricon.

Okay, come on, said Abhyartha.

Look at him one hand is throwing the rice grains and the other hand is eating the rice, said Abhyartha.

You are making fun out of me, said Apricon.

It's okay Apricon, you are a chef now, said Aayun.

Now, I will gonna make you a fruit juice, said Apricon.

How do you gonna prepare it? Said Aayun.

I will gonna add some fruits and water and then grind it. Just I will gonna press this button and this is called sugarless juice, said Apricon.

It tastes good buddy, said Aayun.

Thank you, said Apricon.

Apricon, are you interested in studying? Said Aayun.

Today I want to learn about numbers, said Apricon.

Okay, I will teach you then, said Aayun.

Appa, I want to buy kids truck to Apricon, said Aayun.

For what? Said Bharath.

I want to make him happy, said Aayun.

Okay then, said Bharath.

Apricorn, it's a gift for you, said Aayun.

What's this, said Apricon.

Wow! It's a driving vehicle, I had dreamt of it, said Apricon.

Let's have a ride, said Aayun.

See press this green colour button to drive and press this

red colour button to stop okay, said Aayun.
Hurrah! I drove this vehicle, said Apricon.

CHAPTER TWO

TRAVEL THROUGH
THE WISDOM

In a quiet town where dreams took flight,
Three young minds burned bright at night.
Not through books, nor rules so tight,
But through the stars and endless light.

Their guide, a man both wise and bold,
Dr. Aardhaman, with tales untold.
Not in walls of chalk and dust,
But 'neath the sky, where knowledge thrust.

"Science," he said, "is not just read,
But felt, explored, and molded ahead.
A question sparked, a mind set free,
That's the path to mystery."

They built, they showed, they tried for future,
Like rockets learning how to soar.

A vision to touch the heavens wide,
The runners built with endless pride.

The final day, their operation shone,
Proof of how their minds had grown.
Not just students, but explorers,
Chasing dreams beyond their 'queen' and 'runners.'

As stars above began to gleam,
Dr. Aardhaman, spoke of one last dream
"The universe calls, and so you must,
Not with fear, but endless trust."

Aayun, come here, your summer holidays got over. Tomorrow we'll gonna do admission to your sixth standard okay, said Bharath. Okay Appa, said Aayun.

Hello students, this is your first class for your grade sixth. Guys, all of you should learn well okay, said the teacher.

Okay sir, said the students.

Hey, your Apricon is nice actually, said Banmith (Aayun's friend).

Thank you, said Aayun.

These girls are pretty I will gonna sit with them, said Apricon.

What are you talking about, you idiot, come here this is why you are coming to the school for this purpose, said Aayun.

No... said Apricon.

Students see here I'm your mathematics teacher, today we'll gonna learn about multiplication tables using songs and rhymes and you should follow after me okay.

Sure teacher, said the students.

Apricon, come will go to home now, class is got over, said Aayun.

Okay come on, said Apricon.

Apricon, what you are doing there? Said Abhyartha.

He is watching television, said Aayun.

Hey, where are you going man? Said Aayun.

Watch this, said Apricon.

What's this? Creepers on your head like a crown. Palm leaves all over the body, said Aayun.

Are you a miss universe now! Said Aayun.

Did you saw it on the TV? Said Abhyartha.

Yeah, said Apricon.

That's impressive, said Aayun.

Okay come on, throw those stuff to the dustbin.

So students, see here we are learning mathematics through augmented reality. It's just like an interactive learning session. Immediately after that you will be having speed math challenges with time limit. Whoever wins, there is a price for that, said the teacher.

And the time starts now...

That's the correct answer.

Wow! Apricon, you are the winner of today's challenge, said the teacher.

Okay students, I will gonna distribute colourful flash

cards to practice tables and formulas. In home you can practice guys, said the teacher.

Okay students now we are in shopping mall, do whatever you wanna purchase, then after that you need to calculate discount, total bills and savings okay, said the teacher.

Okay teacher, said the students.

Good morning students, I'm handling political science today and I'll gonna teach you about fundamental duties and fundamental rights.

See here students, under fundamental duties you should respect the national anthem and you should give respect to the national flag okay, said the teacher.

Okay teacher said the students.

And under fundamental rights, students you have the right to education and right against exploitation. And inform children under fourteen that, you guys should not work under factory or any other hazardous work, got it.

Okay, teacher.

Hello students, I'm your history teacher and I will be teaching you history through artificial intelligence here. I would be teaching about kings, their coins, and their social, political and economic life. Here images wood appear about the kings through metaverse. So each and every week of the school day, will go to historical place, there we would be learning about art and culture, about its architecture, the battles they fought. Every week, there would be a drama about Indian National movement, this is the effective way you can study through. So guys tomorrow there will be a test about coins we would be providing you a paper coins, so based on that you should identify the coins from which dynasty it has been came, said the teacher.

Okay teacher, said the students.

Hey everybody, I'm your geography teacher. Today we'll be dealing with earthquakes, volcanic eruptions and oceanography, said the teacher.

First of all, dear student's earthquake caused by the movement of tectonic plates beneath the earth crust. You can watch through this metaverse and you can experience also.

Ohh, that's so cool, said the students.

With regard to volcanic eruptions, here I have created mountain like structure using wood and then a reddish orange like liquid will come out from this and I'm using centrifugal pump and motor to pull out the magma and ashes. This is how you should connect your mind, so that you could able to retain in your brain, said the teacher.

It's so cool, said Apricon.

Tomorrow we'll head towards beach, there we would be learning about oceanography and continental drift theory, said the teacher.

Okay teacher we are eager to see those stuff, said the students.

Here on water, I have made continents on water, you can observe that, how the present South America being detaching from Africa by showing zig-saw fit, said the teacher.

This continental drift theory model seems to be very effective to learn, said the students.

Don't do anything to my friends, are you done with head louse eating, come here, you little thief, said Aayun.

'Eyes gleaming with mischievous, but the kind of knowing and taunting smile that speaks volumes.'

Okay, come Aayun, said Apricon.

Hello guys, I'm your physics teacher, today we would be learning about solar systems, said the teacher.

Guys, all of you wear this oculus, to explore planets, moons and asteroids in a 3D environment, said the teacher. Now I will be asking you questions. Where is our planet? that's my question, said the teacher.

The planet which is in third place is our earth, said Aayun. Good Aayun, said the teacher.

See here students I have created mechanical orrey to study planetary motion, said the teacher.

That's so cool, said Apricon.

Hey buddy, why you are sucking it up? That's not a juice, it's a chemical solution, spit it up, said Aayun.

And this one looks like a mango juice, said Apricon.

Stay away from it, you idiot, you are in a lab now, said Aayun.

Okay, said Apricon.

So students as a part of a biology concept, today we are heading towards medical institute there we would be dealing with human biology and physiology in anatomy department and you will get a clear view, said the teacher. Well students, I'm a professor from the department of anatomy and I would be teaching you brief concepts about nervous system, circulatory system and digestive system and we are using AI for better understanding like in heart pumps blood carrying Oxygen and nutrients is it okay for you, said the professor.

Okay sir, said the students.

So students all the very best for your board exams, do well, said the teachers.

Thank you teacher, said the students.

So Aayun, what you are interested to study further? I mean for your intermediate course and for Apricon as well, said Bharath.

Appa I'm interested in science, said Aayun.

I'm also, said Apricon.

Okay then, tomorrow will be your admission to that stream, said Bharath.

Okay Appa, said Aayun and Apricon.

And one more thing guys, apart from studies if you are interested to play some sports, you can continue with that okay, said Bharath.

Okay Appa, said Aayun.

Hey, you thief, where did you get this cooling glass and why you are showing off in college premises? Said Aayun.

It's from our professor chamber said Apricon. Go and kee it back right now, said Aayun.

Wearing this cooling glass appears to be very cool, how

does it works? Said Aayun.

Hey you fool, it's on the basis of reflection, absorption and transmission of light and heat, said Apricon.

And it protects you from UV-radiation and heat, said Aayun.

See how I taught you, said Apricon.

That's so cool, now can you go and give it back there, said Aayun.

My handsomeness just vanished right now, okay I will go now, said Apricon.

Aayun, do you know anything about Gauss's law, said Apricon.

It is particularly useful for calculating electric field in cases with high symmetry, said Aayun.

Thank you, I was testing you, said Apricon.

Hahaha... said Aayun.

Switch on that light buddy, said Aayun.

Okay, said Apricon.

I thinking like how power distribution would happen and how they could able to make? Said Apricon.

They made it possible through Kirchhoff's law, said Aayun.

Yeah I got it buddy, said Apricon.

Hey what's in your hand, said Apricon.

It's a compass, said Aayun.

Are you navigating? Said Apricon.

No buddy, said Aayun.

I have a question brother, how does it works? Said

Apricon.

Actually, it aliens with earth magnetic field, then pointing towards magnetic north, said Aayun.

Hey, what do you mean by magnetic field? And how does it occurs buddy? Said Apricon.

It is primarily due to the motion of molten iron and nickel in the outer core in which it generates electric currents, said Aayun.

Wait. Wait. What do you mean by core... said Apricon.

Let me explain you now, assume earth is like a watermelon, the greener part would be crust and the whiter part would be mantle and the last one is red part, assume it like a core. These are all components of earth buddy, said Aayun.

I wanna eat watermelon now, so that I could eat core, said Apricon.

Hahaha... said Aayun.

Hey, how this power generation do happen? Said Aayun.

In our country, majority of the power generation done through coal. Thermal power plants is being used for this process, said Apricon.

What will gonna happen after that? Said Aayun.

Fuel combustion do takes place there. I mean coal burns in the boiler to heat water. Then after that, water turns into high-pressure system, then turbine rotation do happen through turbine blades and the turbine do drive the AC generator and this process is called electricity generation.

Wow! Awesome man, said Apricon.

Apricon come here, will go to hospital today, said Aayun.

For what? Said Apricon.

Our, grandmother's hand got fractured, said Aayun.

Then hurry up, said Apricon.

How she has been diagnosed? Said Apricon.

Using X-rays, said Aayun.

How do they discovered that? Said Apricon.

Wilhelm Roentgen, he was a German physicist, while experimenting with cathode rays using a crooks tube, he noticed a mysterious invisible radiation that could pass through objects. He observed that these rays could penetrate human flesh, but not bones creating shadow like images on photographic plates. He named them X-rays, said Aayun.

Ohh, that's so cool, said Apricon.

Apricon, come here, how am I looking? Said Aayun.

You are lesser handsomer than me, said Apricon.

Come and see the mirror, I let you know, said Aayun.

Why am I into this mirror? Said Apricon.

It's because of your reflection, said Aayun.

Can't we live without science, said Apricon.

Point of discussion may be, said Aayun.

Apricon, come will go to farm field right now, said Aayun.

Yeah sure, come on, said Apricon.

This sun tend to make me discomfort and urge to close the eyes, said Apricon.

I think you are a photophobic, said Aayun.

Okay, let me ask you a question. How this sun produces energy? Said Apricon.

Well it happens through nuclear fusion. It is the process in which two light atomic apricons I mean nuclei combine to form a heavier Apricon, I mean nucleus, releasing a tremendous amount of energy like a Hydrogen bomb, said Aayun.

Are you kidding me, said Apricon.

I'm just explaining buddy, said Aayun.

I hate chemistry, said Apricon. Why you are saying like this, do you know? It is fundamental, said Aayun.

What's the use of it my buddy? Said Apricon.

For instance, if you take the concept of solutions you can see wider applications, said Aayun.

Go on, said Apricon.

For example, saline solutions are used in hospitals to treat dehydration, solutions are crucial for manufacturing products like paints, dyes, detergents. Alloys like brass and steel are solid solutions used in construction. In water purification, reverse osmosis is based on the principle of osmosis in solutions. Fertilizers are dissolved in water to enhance plant absorption, said Aayun.

Ohh, gosh! These many uses, said Apricon.

Chemistry is everywhere, it's in everyday life, said Apricon.

Aayun, how this iron could be extracted, said Apricon.

There is a process for that, we can learn through metallurgy, said Aayun.

Aayun, how we're evolved like me and you, said Apricon.

I think we're evolved through you only, said Aayun.

Hahaha... you guys are evolved through me, said Apricon.

May be, I don't know exactly, but we have a theory which was explained by our professor, won't you remember, said Aayun.

Explain it now, said Apricon.

Darwin's theory of Evolution, in which it explains 'how species evolve overtime due to variations and environmental pressures,' said Aayun.

It seems like it evolved through me, said Apricon.

Hahaha... said Aayun.

Okay, let's go home now, said Aayun.

Okay then, said Apricon.

Let's have dinner guys come on, said Abhyartha.

So you guys have done with your intermediate studies, what you are interested to study further? Said Bharath.

Appa, I have decided to study Astronautical engineering, said Aayun.

That's so cool, said Bharath.

Then I must clear the entrance exam, said Aayun.

Do some preparations for that, said Bharath.

Okay Appa, said Aayun.

So, what do you wanna become? Said Bharath.

I want to become an astronaut, said Aayun.

But, you are the only kid in our family, said Abhyartha.

Don't worry Amma, Apricon is there, said Aayun.

Let us allow him to do what he wants to do, said Bharath.

Then what about Apricon, said Abhyartha.

Once if I'm done with this entrance examination and admission, then the place where in I get an admission, I do approach the institute through a small test for him. If he gets more than 50 percent, then there is an admission for him, said Aayun.

So you have decided the test for him, not the institute, said Abhyartha.

Hahaha... said Aayun.

Okay Apricon, I will give test series daily and you should ask me questions okay, said Aayun.

For physics what we will do is, we'll focus on concepts, derivations and problem-solving and need to solve previous year question papers and advanced problems, said Aayun.

Okay then, what about chemistry? Said Apricon.

For chemistry we'll read basic concepts along with numerical practice and reaction mechanisms.

For Mathematics, here concept clarity and problem solving is a must, said Aayun.

And finally we'll make a short notes for revision, said Apricon.

Aayun, today it's your entrance exam, do well, said Bharath.

Thank you Appa, said Aayun.

Apricon, what you are doing! said Abhyartha.

Swinging, said Apricon.

Bharath, come here, look at him, what he is doing, said

Abhyartha. He has tied that rope on to his neck, said Abhyartha.

I will gonna untie his neck, said Bharath.

See Apricon, if you feel like want to swing, I will make a swing for you okay, I'll help you to play, said Bharath.

Wait for a second buddy and its ready, come here, said Bharath.

Aayun come here, give him a push, said Bharath.

How I'm swinging here? How could it be possible? Said Apricon.

When you try to swing, you gonna create a pendulum motion, as I push you, you will gonna increase your kinetic energy. Gravity and a resistance slow you down, but pushing you at the right moment keeps you going. The highest points of the swing have maximum potential energy while the lowest points has maximum kinetic energy, said Aayun.

Ohh my god, whole physics behind swinging, said Apricon.

Aayun, you have cleared the exam, tomorrow will get an admission to that institute, said Bharath.

Hello dear students, welcome to our Indian institute of technology, all I wanted to say make use of time judiciously, have fun, study well and succeed in your mission, said Aardhaman (Astronautical professor).

Inauguration day got over, come on let's go to hostel now, said Aayun.

Okay, come on, said Apricon.

Give it back my stuff... Give it back... said Banmith.

What happened to you actually? Said Aayun

I was having shower, somebody has actually stolen my clothes, said Banmith.

Who is that thief? Said Aayun.

Do you want me to search? Said Aayun.

Yeah, said Banmith.

What are you doing man? Said Aayun.

It's pretty cool clothes, who is roaring there? Said Apricon.

You little thief, why you did like this, said Aayun.

I bet you won't be asking this clothes, do you? Said Apricon.

Give it to me, said Aayun.

Okay, better luck next time, said Apricon to himself.

Actually somebody has exchanged your clothes by mistake, when you are hanged out these clothes there, said Aayun.

Okay, thank you buddy, said Banmith.

Hello guys, welcome to our first class, said professor Aardhaman.

So, let us discuss about the first concept Astrodynamics, in that we'll gonna deal about orbital mechanics and Kepler's law. So what are your expectations in these concept? Said Aardhaman .

Professor what do you mean by orbital mechanics? Said Aayun.

So, Orbital mechanics is the study of how objects move

under gravity, particularly in space. It is based on Kepler's law which describe planetary motion around a central body like the sun or earth.

How many laws are there under Kepler's law? Professor is this the orbits are perfect circles? Said Banmith.

There are three laws. For your second question answer is no. 'Orbits are not perfect circles but ellipses, I mean flattened circles with the sun at one of the two foci of the ellipse' and this explains the Kepler's first law of planetary motion.

Professor is their speed, I mean is planets speed remains to be same when it is closer to the sun or farther, said Aayun.

No Aayun, planets move faster when they are close to the sun (Perihelion) and slower when they are farther (Aphelion) said Aardhaman.

Why is this so professor? Said Aayun.

'This is due to the conservation of angular momentum' and this explains Kepler's second law, said Aardhaman.

Professor, could you tell us about Kepler's third law of planetary motion, said Apricon.

Kepler's third law 'shows a universal relationship between the time a planet takes to orbit and its distance from the sun,' said Aardhaman.

Professor, where it could be useful I mean these Kepler's laws, said Aayun.

It has wider applications like in calculating satellite orbits around earth, predicting planetary positions and space mission planning like in moon landings, said Aardhaman. Moving further, Newton's law of Universal Gravitation and it says that "Everything in the universe pulls on everything else but with the force. This force depends on mass and distance," said Aardhaman.

Professor, you mean, is bigger objects pull more strongly, said Apricon.

And that means, more masses equal to stronger gravity, said Aayun.

Exactly, said Aardhaman.

What about distance? Said Banmith.

Objects that are farther apart pull less, I mean more distance is equal to weaker gravity, said Aardhaman.

Do you know Newton's Apple story guys? Said Apricon.

No, go on, said Aayun and Banmith.

One day Newton was sitting under an apple tree at his home in Wools Thorpe, England. He saw an Apple fall to the ground and wondered "Why do apple always fall straight down? Why don't they move sideways or upwards?"

This simple question led him to think that the same force pulling the Apple down must also be acting on the moon, keeping it in orbit around earth. And this was told by our teachers, when we were in school days, said Apricon.

Well said Apricon, said Aayun and Banmith.

Do you know guys what would I have been done instead of Newton, said Apricon.

No, go on, said Aayun and Banmith.

I would have eaten that fallen apple and might have saved his discovery of gravity, said Apricon.

Hahaha... said Aayun and Banmith.

So, we'll move on to the next concept guys, that is Satellite orbits and trajectories, said Aardhaman.

A satellite is an object that moves around a planet isn't it professor? Said Aayun.

Exactly, it's like the moon around earth or like earth around sun, said Aardhaman.

Is there any types of orbits professor, said Apricon.

Yeah there are many, said Aardhaman.

Is there any use of satellite orbits in-real life? Said Apricon.

Yeah, for instance, it is used for navigation, it track storms for military use, for sending probes to planets as a space missions, said Aardhaman.

Professor, why do satellites won't fall, said Banmith.

Because there is a forces acting on satellites such as gravity keeps it in orbit and centripetal force which prevent it from falling, said Aardhaman.

By the way continue with the orbits professor, said Apricon.

Yeah, first one, circular orbit, where in the satellites move in a perfect circle around the planet and the speed remains constant here, then the next one is elliptical orbits, here the satellite follows an ellipse with the central planet at one focus. And the next one is low earth orbit, where in satellite orbit at 200 to 2000 km altitude.

Moving on geo-stationery orbit, where in the satellite orbits exactly once per day and stays fixed over one spot on earth, usually the altitude ranges from 35,786 km above earth and the last one is polar orbit, where in the satellite passes over both poles as the Earth rotates beneath it and covers the entire planet in multiple orbits, said Aardhaman.

Okay let me ask you a question now, under which orbit, satellite move very fast, said Aardhaman.

It's in low earth orbit, because the mass is very close and the distance is short, said Apricon.

Excellent, said Aardhaman.

Professor, I have a doubt, what will happen if a satellite moves too fast? said Aayun.

Nice question, we'll study escape and transfer trajectories in order to resolve your question.

If a satellite moves too fast, it can escape earth's gravity and go into space and the minimum speed needed is called escape velocity, said Aardhaman.

Professor, is it possible to change Satellite from one orbit to another? Said Banmith.

Yeah, it's a good question that you have asked, it could be possible through Hohmann Transfer orbit (Changing orbit). Here it involves two burns, I mean speed change, where in first burn moves the satellite into an elliptical transfer orbit and the second burn circulize the new orbit, so that it can be used for moving from Low earth orbit to Geo-synchronous orbit and sending spacecraft to the moon or the Mars, said Aardhaman.

Apricon, what you are doing? Said Aayun.

Since from three days it's a heavy rainfall, my clothes doesn't even dried, that's why I put it on the fire, I mean I set the fire on clothes, said Apricon.

Apricon, are you really my buddy? Said Aayun.

No worries, I will take it back right now, said Apricon.

Professor, interplanetary travel involves sending spacecraft from Earth to other planets in the solar system isn't it? Said Banmith.

Yeah, here what do you wanna know about it? Said Aardhaman.

What does it involves while coming back, said Banmith.

It involves mid-course corrections, where in small engine burns adjust the spacecraft's trajectory and these correct for gravitational influences and ensure precision in arrival, said Aardhaman.

Then what about orbital insertion? Said Aayun.

The spacecraft must slow down using aero braking. It means using the planet's atmosphere to the slow down. It then enters a stable orbit, said Aardhaman.

And what about flyby? Said Apricon.

Flyby using parachutes, airbags or powered descent, said Aardhaman.

It's pretty interesting, said Apricon.

Professor, I have a question, said Aayun.

Go on, said Aardhaman.

How do rockets work? Said Aayun.

Yeah, I was about to discuss that, but you have asked that question exactly to that point, so here I will going to explain you now under 'rocket propulsion.'

Usually rocket propulsion is based on Newton's third law of motion: "For every action there is an equal and opposite reaction." A rocket pushes exhaust gases out and in return, it gets pushed forward. Let me explain you in further depth, a rocket burns fuel called propellant to produce high-speed exhaust gases. These gases are expelled downward, creating an upward thrust, said Aardhaman.

Professor, is there any types of rocket propulsion, said Banmith.

Yeah, we'll go one by one, first one chemical rockets, it uses chemical reactions to generate thrust. It includes solid rockets, where in fuel and oxidizer are mixed in solid form, once ignited, they burn continuously. Then comes the liquid rockets, where in fuel and oxidizer are stored separately and mixed in the engine, where in thrust can be controlled, I mean it can be turned on and off. And the next one is hybrid rockets, where in it's a combination of solid fuel and liquid oxidiser and these are all comes under chemical rockets and the second main one is electric propulsion, uses electric fields to accelerate ions. Then comes the last one nuclear rockets, where in it uses nuclear reactions to heat fuel and create thrust.

Professor, we want to know about structural design of spacecraft, said Aayun.

Before moving on to this, you should know about key requirements for spacecraft structure and here it goes like this, first of all spacecraft structure must be lightweight I mean less weight means less fuel required for launch. Secondly it should be strong and rigid in order to survive the high forces of launch and space travel. Then comes, it should resist temperature extremes, it should give protection against radiation and micro meteoroids and finally it should be able to accommodate mission payloads like scientific instruments, rovers or crew must be safely housed, said Aardhaman.

Professor, what kind of material is used for main spacecraft body and for structural frames? Said Banmith.

It is aluminium alloys, said Aardhaman.

Why those stuff only? Said Aayun.

Because it is lightweight, strong and corrosion resistant, said Aardhaman.

And professor, what are the materials used in load bearing parts and fuel tanks? Said Apricon.

It is Titanium due to heat resistant.

And professor what about satellite spacecraft body panels? Said Aayun.

It is carbon fibre composite because of its ultra-light, high-strength-to-wait-ratio, said Aardhaman.

And the most curious one is astronaut suits, what does it made up of professor? Said Banmith.

It is Kevlar, said Aardhaman.

Professor, what about beryllium, for what purpose are we

using it? Said Apricon.

This is for telescope mirrors and for precision instruments due to good heat dissipation, said Aardhaman.

Professor, in space won't they feel degree of hotness, said Apricon.

Yeah, they do feel, but to overcome that, they are using thermal shields for that and aerogels as a material, said Aardhaman.

Guys, when I will be visiting space, I do take sweater, said Apricon.

Why so? Said Aayun and Banmith.

Once if I feel cold means, I can wear it, said Apricon.

Hahaha... said Aayun and Banmith.

Professor, is they are using any spacecraft frame types, said Aayun.

Yeah, they do use monocoque: one piece, like an aircraft fuselage and light weight framework would be truss structure and the last one is modular structure, said Aardhaman.

Professor under thermal protection system, spacecraft must survive extreme heat and cold in space isn't it? Said Banmith.

Yeah, they do face some challenges of space temperature, where no air in space means no convection, so heat management relies on radiation and conduction, said Aardhaman.

Professor, is there any methods to overcome it? Said

Aayun.

Yeah, through Multi-Layer Insulation, where in it reduces heat loss or gain and it is made of thin reflective films. Next one comes the heat shields, it absorbs and reflect heat during atmospheric entry. Moving on, radiators, it removes excess heat from electronics. Phase change materials, where in it stores excess heat and releases it slowly especially in space suits and in satellites, said Aardhaman.

And professor, how do they block cosmic rays, said Apricon.

It happens through lead or water shielding especially human missions, said Aardhaman.

Okay, said Aayun.

Tomorrow, there would be a practical class for you guys on spacecraft designing and your professor will help you guide in this okay, said Aardhaman.

Hurrah! I will gonna design spacecraft tomorrow, said Apricon.

Good morning guys, said Aardhaman.

Good morning professor, said the students.

Professor, that computer system and all in spacecraft, how do they work and what are all its functions? Said Aayun.

Yeah, actually there is a specific term for that and we call it as avionics, said Aardhaman.

Ohh, that's pretty cool term, said Apricon.

Let me explain it in detail, avionics to the electronic systems used in a spacecraft for navigation, communication, control and data processing. These systems ensure the spacecraft can complete its mission accurately, whether it is orbiting earth, landing on mars or travelling deep into space.

Yes professor, said Banmith.

Now, moving on to its functions, the first and foremost one is guidance system where in, it determines the spacecraft's position and trajectory.

Professor, how could we continuously track the position, velocity and attitude of the spacecraft, said Apricon.

Through navigation system, said Aardhaman.

How it could be possible, said Banmith.

It uses sensors, that's how it is possible, for instance star trackers, it identify stars to determine spacecraft orientation, sun sensors to detect the sun's position for navigation, said Aardhaman.

Professor, is there any sensors to measure rotation and movement, said Apricon.

Through Gyroscope, magnetometer, said Aardhaman.

Professor, how could we able to measure distance for landing and docking, said Aayun.

Yeah, it's possible through radar and LIDAR, said Aardhaman.

Professor when we use to drive a car or bike, first we should change the orientation then we aim towards particular direction, is these things can also be possible in space? Said Banmith.Yeah, it could be possible through control system where in, attitude control adjusts the spacecraft's orientation and orbit control, it changes spacecraft trajectory or altitude, said Aardhaman.

And how does it works professor? Said Banmith. They do follow control method reaction wheels, there spin wheels to adjust spacecraft orientation, said Aardhaman.

Professor, apart from these stuff, is there any alternate way to adjust orientation at free of cost from out of space, said Apricon.Yeah, I got your point, there is a specific control method called Magnetorquers where in, it uses earth's field to adjust orientation applies only for small satellites, said Aardhaman.

Wow! That's pretty amazing, said Apricon.

Professor, how do we communicate suppose if we are in space? said Banmith.

Don't you know? Isn't through phone? Said Apricon.

Hahaha... No, since spacecraft travel far from Earth, they need powerful antennas and precise signals to send and receive data. They uses radio waves to send data between the spacecraft and earth, said Aardhaman.

Professor, how do they manage data storage and transmission, said Aayun.

Usually, spacecraft store data on solid-state memory before sending it to earth. And some use AI and edge computing to process data on board and send results, said Aardhaman.

What about power management in avionics professor? Said Banmith.

They do use solar panels to generate electricity for earth

orbiting, batteries to store power for when the spacecraft is in darkness and radioisotope thermoelectric generators provide energy for space missions, said Aardhaman.

Professor, on earth where heat is transferred by conduction, convection and radiation but what about in space? Said Banmith.

That's a pretty good question by the way, space allows only conduction, where in heat moves through solid spacecraft materials and then the next heat transfer mechanism involved here is radiation where in, it is emitted or absorbed as infrared radiation and finally no convection, said Aardhaman.

Why so professor? Said Aardhaman.

Because space has no air, said Aardhaman.

Hey, you buddy wake up! 'Time to rise and shine before the day slips away!' Tomorrow there is an exam for us, go and revise well guys, said Apricon.

Who is sprinkling water here? Is it a dream? Are you kidding with us, Apricon. You have showered whole water tank of hostel to us, said Aayun and Banmith.

It's not a water, it's a hot water just to keep you warm guys, said Apricon.

Okay buddy, we're just woke up. And come we'll study, said Ayaun and Banmith.

Yep, let's go to class now, said Aayun.

See Aayun, Apricon nodded off unexpectedly, said Banmith.

Hahaha... said Aayun.

Guys, we'll move on to the next topic that is space system and satellites, said Aardhaman.

Professor, what do you mean by space systems? Said Apricon.

Well, it refers to satellites, ground stations and supporting infrastructure, that enable communication, navigation, Earth observation and scientific research. Satellites they do play a key role in telecommunications, GPS weather monitoring and space exploration.

Professor, I have a question, are we using the same or only one satellite for different purposes, said Apricon.

No, we have communication satellite, navigation satellite, Earth observation satellite and scientific and space exploration satellite, said Aardhaman.

Communication satellite, they do transmit TV, radio, internet and phone signals across long distances and provide global internet access and emergency communication, isn't it? Said Banmith.

Yeah, exactly, said Aayun.

Do you know about navigation satellite, that provides positioning and timing data and Earth observation satellite to monitor weather, environment and mapping and finally scientific and space exploration satellites, for this explanation is in the name itself, said Aardhaman.

Okay professor, said Apricon.

Okay guys, moving on to the next concept that is 'pay load integration,' it is a process of attaching satellites, scientific instruments or cargo to a launch vehicle. It ensures proper power, data and structural connection between the payload and the rocket. It uses standardized interfaces for modular and small satellites like cubesats, said Aardhaman.

Professor, what do you mean by cubesats here, said Banmith.

These are miniature modular satellite built in standardised sizes, said Aardhaman.

Is it having any applications? Said Apricon.

Yeah, for instance, scientific research technology testing and in commercial applications, said Aardhaman.

Is there any benefit out of it, from these stuff, said Banmith.

Obviously, it is low cost, I mean it is affordable for university and start up for fast development, it can be built in months instead of years for standardised deployment, it will be useful, said Aardhaman.

Okay professor, said Aayun.

Okay, let's continue with the topic that is modular satellites, these are flexible satellite architectures where, different parts can be swapped or upgraded. It reduces cost and development time for space missions, said Aardhaman.

Professor, I have a question, said Apricon.

Go on, said Aardhaman.

How do we deploy satellites so safely to release them into an orbit, said Aayun.

That's a nice question by the way, we do follow some deployment methods like, payload pairing, where it protects satellite during launch. Spring based deployers, it ejects cube sats into space. Rideshare adapters, it allows multiple small satellites to share a launch. Canistered satellite dispensers where in, it encloses and deploys satellites.

Banmith, where is Apricon, said Aayun.

Don't know, but he was on the way to our neighbours home beside to our college, said Banmith.

Yahooo... it's pretty cool, said Apricon.

Hey, you idiot, what you are doing here? Said Aayun and banmith.

I'm just helping our neighbours to lift up water from this well, said Apricon.

For lifting up water, one should pull the rope and should draw water, but what you are doing? You are in the bucket and drowning, is this would be called as help, said Aayun.

cerenaCome on, let's go, said Banmith.

Aunt and uncle, see you tomorrow. Bye. Bye, said Apricon.

Okay guys, had your breakfast, let's go to class now, said Banmith.

Okay then, we shall move, said Aayun and Banmith.

Hello guys, today we shall discuss about space station technology, said Aardhaman.

Professor, is it like travel station, said Apricon.

No, a space station is a habitable artificial structure in orbit that allows astronauts to live and conduct scientific research for extended periods. It requires advanced life support system, power communication and propulsion systems to function efficiently, said Aardhaman.

What does it made up of? Said Aayun.

That's a good question that you're asked. Usually it is made up of modular components say for instance core module, it provides main habitat and life support laboratory modules for scientific research. Docking modules, where in it allows spacecraft to dock. Airlocks for spacewalks and solar power allows to generate electricity, okay that's it for today's class, and you can disperse now, said Aardhaman.

Hey, what's that, on your lips? Said Aayun.

Am I looking beautiful today? Said Apricon.

Tell me exactly, what happened to you? From where did you stole it, said Aayun.

Let me explain you guys, today I went to girls hostel and they were applying some colouring stuff, so it made me curious to apply, said Apricon.

And this is called lipstick you idiot, said Banmith.

By next time don't try this stuff, you got my point, said Aayun.

What's there on your lips Apricon and why so it's reddish? Said Aardhaman.

Professor, for morning breakfast, I ate some spicy and hot food stuff, that's why it is like that, said Apricon.

Just wipe it out for your afternoon's class, said Aardhaman.

Is that the professor found out? Said Apricon.

Well that could be a part of discussion may be, hahaha... said Aayun and Banmith.

Morning guys, please sit down, today we'll gonna discuss about planetary rovers and autonomous navigation, said Aardhaman.

What do you mean by 'planetary rovers' professor? Said Apricon.

Planetary rovers are robotic vehicles designed to explore the surface of other celestial bodies like Mars, the moon and asteroids.

Do they explore space without human intervention and how so? Said Banmith.

Yes, they do, these rovers are equipped with autonomous navigation, scientific instruments and robotic arms to conduct research without direct human intervention, said Aardhaman.

Why they use rovers for space exploration, said Apricon.

Well that's an interesting question, this is because of its mobility can explore different terrains, due to its autonomous navigation. It do collects soil, rock and atmospheric data for scientific research, said Aardhaman.

Professor, how do planetary rovers navigate? Said Aayun.

That's a pretty good question, a rover uses on board AI and hazard detection systems to navigate along with that, it processes images from cameras to avoid obstacles and it creates 3D terrain maps to plan efficient routes, said Aardhaman.

Professor, how do they identify rock composition, said Aayun.

Nice question buddy, rover uses an instrument called spectrometers to extract rock and soil samples, they do use drills and sample collection tools. Weather sensors where in, it measures temperature, wind and radiation. Cameras and microscopes captures high-resolution images, Seismometers detects ground vibrations.

Today we'll talk about an interesting topic that is human spaceflight, said Aardhaman.

What are the prerequisites for human spaceflight, said Aayun.

It's a good question that you're asked, human spaceflight requires advanced life support systems, space habitats and extra vehicular activity suits to keep astronauts safe in the harsh environment of space, said Aardhaman.

Professor, what about life support systems there, how it would be? Said Banmith.

There will be subsystems for each and everything, for instance oxygen generation (OGS) where in, it produces breathable oxygen, carbon dioxide removal (CDRA) removes excess carbon dioxide, temperature control system, radiation shielding and waste management system, these terms are all self-explanatory and no need to explain, you got my point, said Aardhaman.

Yes sir, said the students.

Professor, I have a question, why do astronauts perform spacewalks? Said Aayun.

By the way it's an excellent question, spacewalks, allows astronauts to repair spacecraft, conduct experiments and to assemble space structures outside their habitat, said Aardhaman.

Professor, how do astronauts perform spacewalks? Said Banmith.

Well, they do follow prebreathing protocol, where in astronauts breathe pure oxygen to avoid decompression sickness and they do wear EMU spacesuits with the life support system, then after that, they will depressurize the airlock before opening the hatch and then they stay connected to prevent drifting away and then they do perform tasks like repairs, experiments and then finally they will return to the airlock and restore pressure, said Aardhaman.

Professor, about spacesuits, what does it consists of and how does it works? Said Apricon.

By the way it's a nice question, spacesuit consists of primary life support system(PLSS) where in, it provides oxygen, carbon dioxide removal, temperature control, helmet with HUD display where in, it protects head and provides communication, liquid cooling and ventilation garment (LCVG), it regulates astronaut body temperature. Pressurized layers, it maintains suit pressure to prevent decompression. Gloves with exoskeleton, it enhances dexterity in space. SAFER jetpack as small thrusters for emerging self-rescue, said Aardhaman.

Professor, astronauts, do they face any risks in space? Said Aayun.

Yeah, sadly it is yes, astronauts in space do face radiation exposure and microgravity- related health risks, said Aardhaman.

Does it affect on their health? Said Banmith.

Yeah, for instance, effects of microgravity like MuscleAstrophy, bone density loss, fluid shift, vision changes and orientation, said Aardhaman.

Gosh! it hurts me a lot, said Apricon.

Professor, is there any strategies to overcome radiation, said Aayun.

Here it goes like this, first one is water walls where in, water absorbs radiation and is used for shielding and polyethylene panels, it is lightweight and effective for cosmic ray shielding, said Aardhaman.

Professor, by the way, I forgot to ask you, what do you mean by microgravity, said Apricon.

It means "very weak gravity" where, objects experience weightlessness. Here what happens is, astronauts and objects inside a spacecraft float freely, because they are moving at the same speed as the spacecraft.

So guys, this would be the last class. Good luck, said Aardhaman.

I want to take a moment to sincerely thank you for all your dedication, enthusiasm and engagement throughout this course. Your hard work and thoughtful discussions here have made this journey as an enriching experience for everyone, including myself. It has been a pleasure to be part of your teaching journey and we truly appreciate the effort that you put in, said Aayun.

Thank you Aayun and thank you guys, said Aardhaman.

Guys, before we moving back to our home, we do plant some tree species here, said Aayun.

That's a good idea, said Banmith and Apricon.

Ohh my God, it's a pleasant surprise, we are all seeing you after so long said Bharath and Abhyartha.

Happy seeing you all, said Aayun and Apricon.

Have some nap and I'll prepare some delicious food for you, said Abhyartha.

Appa, how is your farming activities going on, said Aayun.

Yeah, it's going well, said Bharath.

So, what you have decided further, said Bharath.

Appa, 'I have always been fascinated by space science and I genuinely want to contribute to this field.' It combines creativity, engineering and innovation, which excites me the most. There are opportunities in research, government projects and even commercial space tourism. With a specialised MS, I will have a competitive edge in this field. I'll prepare for entrance exams, build a strong portfolio and apply strategically. After my MS, I can work in leading space agencies, face startups and research organisations, said Aayun.

But, you are the only one kid to us, we can't live without you, said Abhyartha.

I understand your concerns and I want to ensure that, I make a wise decision, said Aayun.

Anyway, we'll support you, said Abhyartha and Bharath.

Thank you Amma and Appa, said Aayun.

So, once if we done with our MS, what are the additional qualifications to become an astronaut, said Apricon and Banmith.

Well, to this, they do give us a training for piloting experience, military test pilot training. Scuba diving and underwater training for spacewalk simulations and finally we should have excellent physical and mental health, these are essentials, said Aayun.

Ohh, that's a pretty nice things to do, said Apricon and Banmith.

And along with that, we should have some experience in research or space related industries, said Aayun.

Okay. Said Banmith.

CHAPTER THREE

OPERATION RUNNERS

The Reign of the Queen She moves, and the hive hums.
A golden presence, cloaked in scent,
the rhythm of a thousand wings,
the heartbeat of a kingdom in comb and honey.

As long as she lives, they follow-
workers making royaljelly and sweetness,
drones waiting for a fleeting purpose,
queen whispering life into the young.

She is more than a queen; she is the law,
the pulse, the breath, the beginning.
Her touch binds the air with veneration,
her voice is silent, yet all obey.

But time is a quiet thief.
One day, the life will change,

the air will taste of new beginnings,
and in secret, an another successor will rise.

Yet, until that moment,
as long as she breathes,
the hive will dance, the world will turn,
and the kingdom of "RUNNERS" will endure.

Today, our faces lightning up with nostalgia, said Aayun.

Yeah, we're all done with our MS, said Banmith.

Hurrah! Said Apricon.

Tomorrow, we shall meet our professor Aardhaman, said Aayun.

Okay, said Apricon and Banmith.

Professor, how are you? We're back, said Aayun.

I'm fine. Good to see you guys, so finally you guys are done with MS, said Aardhaman.

Thank you professor, said Banmith.

Professor, we came here to discuss some stuff regarding 'space project' and we would like to name it as 'OPERATION RUNNERS' said Aayun.

Well, it's quite interesting, go on, said Aardhaman.

Professor, we would like to grow a fruit crop like strawberry in low Earth orbit and along with that we do conduct research on honey bees reproduction and pollination. If this could happen with the success, then there is a possibility of life with better systems, we might one day grow crops in space habitats for future moon or Mars mission, said Aayun and Banmith.

But, it do comes with the challenges like microgravity, where in plants rely on gravity to direct their roots downward and stems upward. In space, plants adopt by growing in all direction. In microgravity water doesn't flow normally; it forms floating droplets, making traditional watering impossible. Special watering systems are needed. Plants in space are exposed to higher radiation levels, which can affect growth and DNA. Then there is lack of soil, limited light and carbon dioxide, said Aardhaman.

Professor, we are ready for everything, said Apricon.
Professor, you were saying about microgravity, we'll gonna design a spacelab in such a way that strawberry planting in one cabin in a fixed manner where in, we'll gonna use an enclosed system at the base of the root system, where in water cannot float or flow, said Aayun.
Nice idea that you have told, said Aardhaman.
Regarding water issues, we have designed special watering systems like Nano drip irrigation system, where in we'll be using Nano drippers and it should be fixed at the base of the root zone and we have designed a radiation sheets, where in we use water as a shielding material and artificial LED lights and controlled carbon dioxide levels to photosynthesize efficiently, said Banmith.

Hmm... good, said Aardhaman.

And we want to experiment on hydroponic system, said Apricon.

I appreciate your efforts, said Aardhaman.

Professor, you might be getting a doubt like, how do you handle pests and diseases, said Aayun.

For that purpose biotechnology department, they do help us. Here scientists do modify plant DNA to introduce desirable traits like drought tolerance, pest and disease resistance and along with higher nutritional value, said Aayun.

Then what are the propagating material that you are using it for strawberry cultivation? Said Aardhaman.

Through 'RUNNERS' said Banmith.

Professor, here we'll try out both tissue culture and hydroponics, said Apricon.

First we'll conduct tissue culture experiment and then after that field trials on earth. The outcome plants we will use it in the space.

Professor, he is Mr. Jaiswan (scientist from biotechnology department) said Aayun.

Hello nice to meet you sir, said Aardhaman.

It's a pleasure to be here sir, said Jaiswan.

So how do you experiment on tissue culture? Said Aardhaman.

Here, we'll take a strawberry stem, leaves or roots as a plant tissue sample and then the plant tissue is disinfected to prevent contamination. And then we do place a tissue in nutrient rich media inside a sterile container. Then cells do multiply and form an undifferentiated mass called callus. Then we do add hormones to stimulate shoot and root growth. Once if the plants mature, they are gradually introduced to soil condition to check it out under field conditions before moving to the space, said Jaiswan.

Well said, then how do you perform DNA modification? Said Aardhaman.

First of all, we'll take out desired genes and then these are inserted into plant cells using bacteria or a gene gun. Then these modified cells grow into full plants using tissue culture methods as I have explained you earlier, then we do testing and screening, I mean we will check out plant resistance, growth and yield, then we'll go with field trials, said Jaiswan.

It's fantastic, said Aardhaman.

And Mr. Jaiswan, how do you perform hydroponics? Said Aardhaman.

Under hydroponics, plants do grow under nutrient rich water, instead of soil.

It consists of hydroponic system like deep water culture, nutrient solution (like NPK, micro nutrients). We do use pH and EC meters in order to maintain water balance and LED lights for photosynthesis, said Jaiswan.

That's pretty cool, okay go on, said Aardhaman.

And planting material are placed in a growing medium, then the small grown plants are placed in a hydroponic setup and roots absorb nutrients from water, artificial lightning is used to maintain proper growth conditions. Then we do growth monitoring and finally harvesting of produce, said Jaiswan.

Well said Mr.Jaiswan, said Aardhaman.

By the way Aayun, how long does strawberry takes to produce fruits under normal field conditions, said Aardhaman.

Professor, hardly four months, said Aayun.

Don't you think it's too long in space, said Aardhaman.

We will be reducing phases here through biotechnological approaches like tissue culture and micro propagation or through genetic engineering. Sometimes we do use growth regulators for instance cytokinins, which enhances cell division and speed up maturity, said Jaiswan.

So professor, we are conducting research in strawberry farming along with honeybee's reproduction and pollination stuff and we are handling it parallelly in a bifurcated cabin of the space lab, said Banmith.

I'm very impressed, said Aardhaman.

By the way Aayun, I forgot to ask you about the honeybees said Aardhaman.

Professor, she is on the way, said Aayun.

Who is she? Said Aardhaman.

Ohh, very sorry Aayun, bit delayed, said Madhuna.

Professor, meet Ms. Madhuna, she is an entomologist, said Aayun.

Nice to meet you madam, said Aardhaman.

Hello sir, it's my pleasure to be part of this project sir, said Madhuna.

So, professor she will guide us in this journey, said Aayun.

So, Ms. Madhuna tell us about honeybee reproduction process, said Aardhaman.

Well, honeybee reproduction is unique and involves queenbees, worker bees and drones in a highly organised colony structure, said Madhua.

So what do each of these bees play here? said Aardhaman.

I will go one by one, here queen bee is the only fertile female responsible for laying eggs, said Madhuna.

What do you mean by drones here, is this an unmanned Aerial vehicle? Said Aardhaman.

Hahaha... no drones are male bees their sole purpose is to mate with the queen and I left with worker bees, these are sterile females that all care for eggs, larvae and the hive, said Madhuna.

Ohh, it's such a huge work they do here, go on, said Madhuna.

Then after that a young queen leaves the hive for a mating flight. She mates with multiple drones in mid-air, after mating, drones die, said Madhuna.

Why do they die here? Said Aayun.

Because their reproductive organs detach while mating, said Madhuna.

Then what happens to queen after that, said Banmith.

Then the sperm is stored in the queen's spermatheca, enough to fertilize eggs for years, said Madhuna.

What about egg laying and development, said Banmith.

The queen lays up to 2000 eggs approximately per day in hexagonal wax cells. Eggs hatch into Larvae and are fed royal jelly or worker bee food. Queens would emerge in 16 days, workers in 21 days and drones in 24 days, said Madhuna.

What next after that? Said Aardhaman.

Swarming and new colonies do form, said Mudhana.

Ms.Madhuna could you elaborate it please, said Aayun.

When the hives becomes overcrowded, a new queen is raised. The old queen leaves with a swarm to form a new colony, said Madhuna.

So what did you understood by this? Said Madhuna.

So we need to use the fresh swarm for this purpose said Aayun.

As long as the queen is alive we can conduct research, said Banmith.

Exactly... good, said Madhuna.

Okay guys, thank you all for coming here and for your guidance, said Aardhaman.

You are welcome sir, said Madhuna and Jaiswan.

So, guys go and do your preparations stuff, said Aardhaman.

Okay professor, said Aayun, Banmith and Apricon.

Professor, everything regarding space shuttle launch is ready, said Aayun.

Good luck guys, all the very best, said Aardhaman.

Thank you professor, said Aayun, Banmith and Apricon.

"Aayun, this is Bemen (a person from the ground station). You are go for lunch. T-minus 10 seconds and counting."

Aayun is go for launch, said the commander (Astronaut-Shuttle cockpit)

Mission control: "T-minus 5...4...3...2...1... Ignition Lift-off! Aayun, you are clear of the tower."

Pilot (Astronaut): We have lift-off, all systems nominal.

Yahoo... said Apricon.

Veah... haaa... said Aayun.

You idiot, are you a Cosmo phobic, said Apricon.

No, I'm doing well, said Aayun.

Then why are you shouting? Said Apricon.

No I was just chilling, said Aayun.

Hey, come on guys, said Banmith.

Mission control: "Copy, Aayun. Roll program initiated. You're looking good."

Commander: Roll program confirmed. We are now pitching over for ascent trajectory". Mission control: "How are your readings?"

Pilot: "Nominal across the board. Vehicle is stable."

Mission control: "Copy. SRB separation in 3... 2... 1... confirmed."

Commander: "Solid rocket boosters have been separated. Main engine running at 104%."

Mission control: "Aayun, you are go for main engine cut-off (MECO) in 10 seconds."

Pilot: Preparing for MECO.

Mission control: "Main engine cut-off confirmed. External tank separation successful." Welcome to orbit Aayun, Banmith and Apricon.

Commander: "Bemen, Aayun here. We are in orbit! Feels great to be in space!"

Mission control: Enjoy the ride, Aayun we'll begin post insertion checks now.

Ohh my god, I'm floating, it's great to be here, said Apricon.

"Alright team, we're just reached orbit. How's everyone holding up?" said Aayun.

"Feeling good, Aayun, systems are stable. We're entered zero gravity" said Banmith.

"Same here. The views incredible. I can see Earth below its surreal."

"Yeah, it's breath-taking. You don't get used to it, do you? Said Aayun.

"Not at all. It's hard to a wrap your head around how small and fragile everything looks from up here" said Banmith.

"I'm starting the first round of checks on the equipment. Everything looks green so far" said Aayun.

"Good. Let's keep the momentum going we'll need to monitor carefully," said Banmith.

"I'll begin the orbital adjustments, now we'll be on track for the rendezvous in about two hours," said Aayun.

"Agreed, we're in a smooth orbit. Things are going well" said Apricon.

"Alright, let's get to work. We've got a mission to complete and a whole new word to explore!" said Aayun. Come on, we'll go to space lab now, Aayun first you should do planting to the hydroponic system, said Apricon.

These tissue cultured strawberry plants, they are looking nice actually, said Banmith.

So, set the hydroponic system, do planting now, said Aayun.

Do check whether Nano drip is going properly or not, said Apricon.

Yeah, it's done, said Banmith.

Then do switch on the nutrient rich media to let it exactly at the root zone and for other chamber, keep the runners, said Banmith.

Yeah, it's done, said Aayun.

What you are looking through cupola? Said Aayun.

Our home, said Apricon.

Do you miss them? Said Aayun.

Yes I do, said Apricon.

Do you know one thing Aayun, sometimes political crisis, hunger strike, geo-political issue, emergency, health crisis, pandemic, wars, problems and stress do happen on earth, but by here we are just considering only earth as a glowing planet, said Apricon.

Yeah, I do agree for every crisis, there is a solution, so we should analyse and take a good decision to solve and to help mankind, said Banmith.

Guys, parallelly we should set out honey bees reproduction system, come on now, said Aayun.

Okay, said Apricon.

Banmith, you do fix the beehive, said Aayun.

Can you differentiate queen, said Banmith.

The one which is long and large in size that is called Queen, said Apricon.

Then, how you differentiate between workers bee and drones, said Apricon.

In drones, we have the number of ommatidia in the eyes is more as compared to queen and worker bee, said Aayun.

And we are researching Apis cerana here, said Banmith.

It is secreting something, said Apricon.

And that's called 'yellow rain' (honey bees excreta) said Banmith.

Check whether the royal jelly is secreting or not, can you see it through microscope, said Aayun.

Yeah, it's secreting, said Apricon.

From where it is secreting you fool, said Aayun.

From the food gland which is present in worker bees, said Apricon.

Good... I was testing you, said Aayun.

Why this royal jelly is is so important? Said Banmith.

Because it has nutritious value, sometimes it is referred as a bee milk and it is fed to the young larvae, said Aayun.

Guys, release the drones and queen, we'll wait for some time, said Aayun.

Let's see whether any drone has died, said Aayun.

Ohh yes, said Apricon.

Hey guys come on, do monitor pH, said Aayun.

Yeah it's in normal range only guys, said Banmith.

Guys, come here, see the magic here, said Banmith.

Hey that's a robotic butterfly, how did you made this one, it's so cool, said Apricon.

I made it by using carbon fibre, enabling to mimic the delicate and light nature of a real butterfly and I have designed the wings to flap using motors and equipped with camera and microphones and used some small battery to power, said Banmith.

Apricon, control the butterfly system and keep water in front of honeybees, because they do drink water, said Aayun.

Yeah, I'm monitoring, said Apricon.

Wow! You have created a porous layer in this robotic butterfly to drink water efficiently for honey bees, said Apricon.

Thank you Apricon, said Banmith.

Honeybees do dance isn't this a magic, said Apricon.

No... it's a miracle, said Banmith.

Hahaha... said Aayun.

Why this robotic butterfly is in green colour? Said Aayun.

Because honey bees won't recognise red colour, that's why, said Banmith.

Come on guys, flowering has been started in strawberry cabin, said Apricon.

That's good, said Banmith.

Now release the worker bee to the strawberry cabin and see whether it is collecting the pollen or not, said Aayun.

Yeah I'm monitoring and it's collecting pollen.

Okay that's fine, from which part it is collecting pollen? Said Banmith.

The hind legs, said Aapricon.

Come to the honey bee cabin guys, monitor whether workerbees are feeding royal jelly to the larvae, said Aayun.

Yeah its happening, such an amazing creature these are and guys they are self-cleaning by themselves and how disciplined they are, said Banmith.

Aayun, come here, keep an extra beehive so that queen do swarming process, said Apricon.

Yep, it's done, said Aayun.

So far, from this honeybees research, what kind of result are we drawing here guys, said Banmith.

The process of pollination is actually happening through transfer of pollen grains from one plant to another, said Aayun.

Exactly guys, said Apricon.

Guys come on, let's have some food, said Aayun.

Apricon, go and drink water, you did drifted away water, you doesn't even know how to drink water under microgravity, said Aayun.

Over there it's floating, do one thing, you drink half of the water that has floated and remaining stuff I'll try to drink, said Apricon.

You little buddy, said Aayun.

Hahaha... said Banmith.

Guys come here fruit setting has also happened, said Banmith.

And one more thing is that we did trialled out zerograviy for honeybees reproduction on earth before we came into this space, I think that field trials made us possible here.

Wow! We did it, said Aayun and Banmith.

Apricon come here, Banmith will take care of you, you should be careful in each and everything okay, now I'll go and do spacewalks okay.

Careful guys I'm going, said Aayun.

CHAPTER FOUR

THE SPIRID

In the twilight of unknown worlds, a lone astronaut strides into a realm where cosmic shadows dance with light,

A place where fear yields to gentle wonder-A universe that blooms like Aayun's curious dream. Beside him, lifeforms from an outer world glissade,

Their luminous forms whispering secrets of distant galaxies; though fear once clutched his heart at the unknown threshold,

He met their gaze with kindness and the quiet strength of awe. This world unfurls like a fantastical tapestry,

Where micro-gravity sings and the very air shimmers with mystery; each step on this surreal path-a delicate breeze through landscapes that echo the marvels of Wonderland.

He strides softly through gardens of stardust and shifting hues, where each creature's presence is a verse in a numinous,

And the cosmos itself unfolds in a tender dialogue between the familiar pulse of compassion and the thrill of the unknown.

*In that strange and wondrous place, fear dissolves into light,
A silent surrender to the magic of embracing difference; And
like Aayun in his charmed realm, he learns-True adventure
lies in the courage to love what you do not yet know.*

"Alright, I'm out here. The view is incredible! Earth looks so peaceful from up here," said Aayun.

"I know, it's surreal: How's your suit holding up?" said Banmith.

"Everything's good so far. Temperature's stable, oxygen's good. Just double-checking my tether" said Aayun.

"Yeah, good idea. We don't want any surprises. I'm starting to adjust to the weightlessness, but it still feels like a weird floaty feeling" said Banmith.

"Right? I keep bumping into the station. Zero gravity is fun tricky sometimes" said Banmith.

"Tell me about it. How's is it looking on your side?" said Aayun.

"Let's hope everything goes according to plan," said Apricon.

"Yeah, let's just keep an eye on everything. We don't want to make any mistakes up here" said Aayun.

"Agreed. And hey, make sure you take a moments to look around. I don't think we get moments like this often, said Apricon.

Definitely. It's easy to get caught up in the task, you're right. This is something special" said Aayun.

Yeah, you're right, said Apricon.

I'll tell you what, though-once we're done, we need to get back inside quickly. It's a little cold out here; said Aayun. "Noted. Let's finish this and head home. Spacewalks are amazing, but there, no place like inside the station" said Banmith.

Guys, I'm coming, Ohh gosh! something is heading towards us, said Aayun.

Hurry up, first you come inside, said Banmith.

Ahh... something has pulled me up, I'm going away. You guys be careful there, I will be back, said Aayun.

We'll be waiting here, said Banmith.

What happened to Aayun, I'll go and find him now, said Apricon.

Apricon, it's too dangerous there, we'll wait here, and he'll come back for sure, said Banmith.

Hello, is anyone there, anybody here, where am I now? Said Aayun.

I will gonna use voice synthesiser here, we come in peace, who are you? Said Aayun.

I'm SPIRID (An imaginary extra-terrestrial species)

Why did you brought me here? Said Aayun.

You are matter-bound. Limited. Yet you reach beyond your spere. I'm curious to know about you, that's why I brought you here, said Spirid.

"We seek knowledge. We explore to understand the universe" said Aayun.

Ohh that's what you are doing in that orbit, said Spirid.

Can you help us understand your nature? Are your life as

we know it? Said Aayun.

'Life. Energy. awareness. We are the resonance between forces. You are solid echoes.'

Curious echoes, said Spirid.

Come here, I will introduce this world, ohh don't touch it or else you will get scared, said Spirid.

Ohh gosh! It's like a large glowing mushroom, where in it is compressed layer by layer, once if we touch it, it do stands up, ohh these are amazing creatures here, said Aayun.

You want to have food? Said Spirid.

I brought it and I'll have it right now, said Aayun.

So, what you will have for food here? Said Aayun.

We have flower gas and fern nuts, said Spirid.

Ohh, it's interesting, come and show these stuff, said Aayun.

Yeah sure, come on then, said Spirid.

Ohh, it's like a large mass of paper flowers, which is swollen like balloon, said Aayun.

Are you surprised to see these stuff, do you? Here we do burst this flower gas and we do breathing, only this flower gas is enough to survive for many more days. Our body do turns red once if we are insufficient of these flower gas, we do survive as long as this flower gas is alive, said Spirid.

Well it's quite interesting, said Aayun.

Take a look at this stuff here, it's a large fern tree, they do produce nuts, it's very nutritious and delicious as well and we do eat this stuff, said Spirid.

It's an amazing survival system that I have found here, said Aayun.

What's your planet be called? Said Spirid.

Ours's is Earth, what about this one? Said Aayun.

ZOROE (An imaginary outer planet) said Spirid.

It's turning dark, come on, let's go to home, said Spirid.

Your home is beautiful, it's like a rock cave one above the other, said Aayun.

Hey come on kids, running here and there, what's wrong with you kids? Said Spirid.

The Little Spirids, you are so cute... said Aayun to the Little Spirids.

Ohh come on, open your cocoon structure, no hide and seek anymore, said Spirid.

What's this, cocoon? We do produce these golden thread like structure, it surrounds our body, it's like defence mechanism once if some other species do attack on us, said Spirid.

That's pretty cool, said Aayun.

Hey kids come on, come and meet him, he is your uncle. He is an earthling, his name is Aayun.

I brought some strawberry fruits here, do you wanna try kids? said Aayun.

Hmm... it's yummy... said Little Spirids.

Kids, call the Bloomids (Light insects like lifeforms) said Spirid.

Come on Bloomids, dad is calling you all, come light up

here, said Little Spirids.

Ohh, I have never seen this before, said Aayun.

These are like bioluminescent insects, head is like a gem and its swollen thorax produces light, almost the size of coconut and thorax is almost like a diamond structure or shape. It's so cool, said Aayun.

So half of our Zoroe lit up by our Bloomids during dark time, said Spirid.

That's nice actually, said Aayun.

Well, thank you, said Spirid.

What's this, is it raining? Said Aayun.

Did you get afraid of it? Said Spirid.

No... said Aayun.

These are Roanyams (Starfish like creatures), they do fly on air and provides water in the form of rain, said Spirid.

From where do they collect water? Said Aayun.

Beside to our habitat, there is another creatures, from there they do collect water, said Spirid.

Hey come on guys, hurry up, said Spirid.

What's that? Said Aayun.

These are Raakus (A crawling animal) said Spirid.

These are pretty amazing, their body structure is like a truck with the crawling legs as wheels with only one eye, said Spirid.

What they will do here, said Aayun.

They do collect these rainy water on their back and give it to us to keep our home cool, said Spirid.

Ohh gosh! That's so incredible stuff I have never seen this

before, said Aayun.

Ahhh! What's that? Said Aayun.

These are Lumoes (Bioluminescent plants like creatures) said Spirid.

It's like a small plants and the entire plant is covered by a thin layer of bulb like structure, said Aayun.

Do you know the speciality of it? These do light up when our shadow do touches on them and once the shadow disappear, they do lit off, said Spirid.

It's a miracle planet actually, said Aayun.

'Your presence disturbs the flow. But your curiosity sings. A fragile melody in the void,' said Spirid.

"Then we have much to learn from each other," said Aayun.

Exploring to outerworld is change. Change is learning. Will you risk unmaking what you know? Said Spirid.

"Yes, that is why we left our world to find what lies beyond," said Aayun.

Then the Zoroe welcomes you, said Spirid.

We are explorers from distant world. We seek knowledge not conflict, said Aayun.

We cooperate in other ways, said Spirid.

Are you a single being or many minds acting as one? Said Aayun.

We are many. We are one. The hire speaks through us. We see through thousands of eyes. You... alone in your skulls. Is it not lonely? Said Spirid.

"We have each other. We find meaning in connection,

even as individuals," said Aayun.

Curious, said Spirid.

'You drift like living auroras, their body's irridescent light and filaments of scintillating energy. You guys neither solid nor entirely ethereal an-ever shifting tapestry of colours flowing like liquid silk through the void and your forms is like a gentle grace of ocean waves, each movement echoing unspoken harmony with the Cosmos.'

"When they gather, they do not stand in lines or circles but form spirals moving in an intricate celestial dance, as if echoing the galaxies that birthed them. In the vast silence of space, they do not conquer, they do not destroy- they simply exist, a living testament to the elegance of the Cosmos".

You are like an Astrovore, said Aayun.

I didn't get your point, could you describe it further? Said Spirid.

And hear it goes like this...

'Cosmic floaters of the void. Drifting through the endless void of space, you are living radiance of celestial energy. Your bodies are near perfect Spheres, smooth and pulsating with a soft, otherworldly luminescence. Swirls of Deep blues, radiant violets and shimmering silvers ripple across their form, as if the very essence of a enable of a celestial veil is trapped beneath your transluscent' said Aayun.

Ohh, that's great, go on, said Spirid.

From the underside of your spherical bodies extend four

elongated limbs, jointed and graceful, each ending in delicate, multi-segmented appendages that can grasp, manipulate or fold seamlessly against your form when not in use along with your cocoon like structure for defence. These limbs shimmer with energy, subtly altering their density to stabilizers moving through different gravitational fields.

'Unlike conventional creatures, you do not rely on wings or propulsion system. Instead, you guys do generate powerful gravitational waves, bending space itself to travel effortlessly across the Cosmos. With a single shift in your internal energy, you can slingshot yourselves through the void, riding the currents of cosmic radiation, skipping across the fabric of space-time like a river cross bridge.'

Your luminescence is not merely for beauty, it is power embodied. The energy that flows through you can disrupt magnetic fields, absorb stellar radiation and even bend light around your form. When fully charged you can unleash controlled bursts of plasma, for bringing brief corridors of energy through which they vault between planets with ease.

You are a silent, radiant traveller, defying the limits of biology, moving between world as effortlessly as a breeze through your defence like cocoon structure and you are a cosmic wanderers along with your existence is a testament to the boundless wonders hidden amount the stars, said Aayun.

You have described me so nicely, thank you very much, said Spirid.

Spirid you have talked about other habitat isn't it? Said Aayun.

Yeah... said Spirid.

Shall we go and see them, said Aayun.

But you should be careful there okay. Their main head is quite dangerous but not the subordinates, said Spirid.

But I will follow your rules, said Aayun.

Okay then, said Spirid.

And promise me that you should help me for reaching out my space shuttle, they might be waiting for me, said Aayun.

Yes I do, said Spirid.

CHAPTER FIVE

THE VEGGOES

Through endless void, so vast, so deep,
A lone man propelled, his fate to keep.
Beyond the world he once called home,
In silent dark, he dared to roam.

Yet cruel hands of doom took hold,
A weary heart, a body cold.
His breath grew weak, his vision dim,
The stars no longer shone for him.

But kindness soared on cosmic waves,
A Spirid came, a life to save.
With gentle hands and faithful grace,
He brought him back to 'runners' and existence.

Now Earth below and celestial dome above,
He wakes once more to light and love.
A tale of stars, of loss and flight,
And how the kind bring back the light.

Ahhh... What is coming out of this mound like structures here? said Aayun.

These are called VEGGOES (An imaginary extra-terrestrial species of otherkind). They do sleep inside mounds, said Spirid.

A lifeform of lop-sidedness. Its head is smooth and rounded, a polished dome with a single, unblinking eye at its centre. The eye is vast, deep, shifting in like liquid metal, absorbing light rather than reflecting it. Its body is perfect square, rigid yet strangely sturdy, as though carved from calcium like substances. The surface pulses with faint bioluminescent veins, shifting in pattern as if displaying thoughts in waves of glowing sphere. The weight of its form give it an imposing presence, yet it moves with a grace that contradicts its shape. From the sides of its body extend two arms-one short, one unnervingly long? The smaller hand twitches with delicate precision like a thorn like of structure, manipulating strange stuff or tracing biological sequences in the air.

The longer arm drapes nearly to the ground fingers elongated and multi-jointed, capable of reaching across distances that seen unnatural for a being of its size.

Its legs are sturdy, jointed in a way that suggests it evolved for traversing harsh landscapes. Every step it takes leaves a faint engraving in the dust, glowing briefly before fading, as if the planet remembers its touch.

They are having something, what's that? Said Aayun.

That's a fruit nut, it's like a nutritional drink to them, said Spirid.

Ohh gosh! What is it doing? It's manipulating the atmosphere around us, said Aayun.

I'm here, said Spirid.

It is drawing what it needs, my blood samples... said Aayun.

Actually it is collecting your blood samples through a spine like structure which is attached to its hand, it is just making sure that whether you are healthy or not, said Spirid.

What is this doing? Said Aayun.

Through your blood samples cells rearranged, corrected and optimised. They will do some research on that, don't worry, said Spirid.

The head of Veggoes, he is heading towards us, said Spirid.

Who is this creature? Said Veggoes.

He is an earthling, said Spirid.

Look like he knows technology very well, said Veggoes.

Yes, he does, said Spirid.

I'll keep this creature here, said Veggoes.

No you can't. I'm responsible for him and I brought him here just to show our world, said Spirid.

I'm head to this habitat and you should obey my words, said Veggoes.

It's not even in your dream also, said Spirid.

We are heading towards our habitat, you can leave now,

said Spirid.

Here you are, tell me where you did hide him? Let him go, said Spirid.

You can't, said Veggoes.

He is mine, you can't even fly and you guys can only do research on him and apart from that you can't draw anything from him. We are also a creature and he is also like one of us. If I shouldn't have brought him, this wouldn't been the issue, said Spirid.

The Battle of rivalry: The fold begins to distort, space buckling as the two Astrovores exert their power. For the first time, I witness something. They never expected-conflict between beings of pure energy. The forerunner bickering aggressively, its dark blue light shifting to deep crimson.

They are not ready. And their choice is their own.

I won't allow you, said Veggoes.

Okay now I'll take a step further. Little Spirids and the Little Veggoes come over here guys, we should rescue Aayun. It's very important guys, said Spirid.

Ohh come on don't tie me up, said Veggoes.

And you are deserved to be like this, feel the pain, said Spirid.

Ohh, my dear Aayun, here you are, did you get hurt? Is he did something to you? Said Spirid.

No, he had just kept me in this place, said Aayun.

Okay come on, we'll move to our habitat, said Spirid.

Ohh you, little Spirids and the Little Veggoes, thank you

very much for helping me out from this, said Aayun.

You are welcome Aayun uncle, said the Little Spirids and the Little Veggoes.

I'll gonna miss you all. With your permission can I take the soil samples over here, said Aayun.

Yeah, sure you can, said Spirid.

We are heading towards your planet, said Spirid.

Yeah, we shall go. Bye. Bye kiddos, said Aayun.

I'm leaving, said Aayun.

We'll gonna miss you, uncle Aayun, said Little Spirids.

'A pathway of golden light forms ahead of them, leading back to their solar system, back to home. You will return. The universe does not wait for the slow to awaken.'

We are back, said Spirid.

Thank you very much, you are the kindest I have never seen, though we are from different worlds, said Aayun.

Its okay, first you go inside. I'll gonna miss you a lot. I'm heading back right now, said Spirid.

Okay take care. Bye. Bye, said Aayun.

'The Spirid finally dissolves into the distant currents of space, it's glow merging with the cosmic tides. It is gone.'

'But the feeling of it left behind remains.'

'A sense of something watching over them. Not as a god, not as a guardian angel, but as a presence that cared, in whatever way something so vast, so unknowable, could.'

Ohh, come on Apricon, have some food and he will be back for sure okay, said Banmith.

'Crew module floats in the vast silence of space, it's

interior dimly lit by control panels and flickering monitors. For hours-day, even the crew inside has been waiting, scanning the void, hoping against all odds.'

And finally-the hatch opens. Aayun went into the crew module, his face exhausted, but smiling.

Banmith and Apricon, before they can even say word, arms rap around them.

"You scared the hell out of us"

"We thought we lost you!"

"Where the hell were you?" said Banmith and Apricon.

"You wouldn't believe me if I told you," I'll explain you each and everything okay, first will head to our home, said Aayun.

CHAPTER SIX

BACK TO THE WOMB

He went. He wedged. He lost ember of himself along the way.

But with each hope, he rose again, the essence of pursuit on distant world tugging him surging with the succor of Spirid.

And when at last he stood before the threshold, broken but unbroken, the 'runners' opened a door not just to a place, but to a belonging, a love that had waited beyond the celestial sphere. He is back to the earth.

The countdown begins here. "Alright everyone. Re-entry sequence is initiated. Heat shields are primed. We're going to make it" said Aayun.

"Atmospheric pressure increasing. G-forces... we'll start filling it soon" said Banmith.

"All shields are green, commander. Heat shields are holding. Just need to ride this out" said Astronaut engineer.

"We have been through worse. This is just final stretch" said Aayun.

"Hold on... it's getting stronger. Brace for impact" said Apricon.

"We're in the thick of it now. Just a few more minutes" said astronaut engineer.

"Stay with me everyone. Just breathe. Focus. We're almost there" said Banmith.

And outside, the glow of re-entry begins to intensify, flames looking the edges of their heat shield. The heat is unbearable, but they know it's necessary.

"I never thought I would feel this much heat again. It's like we're on fire," said Apricon.

"Better than floating out there in the void, right? Said Banmith.

"But I'll take the fire over the void any day" said Aayun.

As the minutes drag on, the shaking begins to subside. The atmosphere to stabilize and the screaming winds outside start to calm. The ship slows its descent. The G-forces easing. They're nearly through the worst of it.

"We have got it. We've made it through the worst of it. Heat shields are holding steady". "We were really going to make it, aren't we? We're home" said Aayun.

Outside the blue sky of earth grows clearer, now under control. They begin to descend into the atmosphere, the ground approaching below, lush and green beneath them. The crew is on edge, but they're seeing Earth again, finally.

"This is it, team. Just a little more. We're going to touch down soon," said Aayun.

"I've never seen anything so beautiful" said Apricon.

"I don't think anyone will ever look at a blue sky the same way again" said Banmith.

No, we won't. We're going to land and we're going to walk on that soil. And when we do... We're going to take a deep breath" said Aayun.

"We made it" said Banmith.

"We're really home" said Apricon.

Can't believe it... We're back, said Banmith.

Back on earth. Mission control erupts into cheers. Engineers embrace. Families watching the broadcast into tears. Across the world, news station announce the impossible.

"RUNNERS crew survives against all odds!"

The mission that was almost lost has turned into a miracle.

How are you guys, happy to see you all, said Bharath and Abhyartha.

I'm very proud of you guys, said professor Aardhaman.

Thank you sir, without your efforts, it wouldn't have been possible, said Aayun.

Go and have some rest guys, said professor Aardhaman.

Sure sir, said Banmith and Apricon.

Hey, you're saying something about the Spirid girl isn't it? Said Banmith.

So sorry, I forgot to tell you that Spirid girl wants to

marry Apricon and she had also sent me some letters for her proposal to Apricon, said Aayun.

No... I am not at all interested, said Apricon.

Hahaha... And smiling...

As the Astronauts unbuckled their harnesses and prepare to disembark, they exchange glances-exhausted, but triumphant. Their journey isn't over, but this chapter, the one of survival of overcoming impossible odds, is finally complete. They step towards the door to face the world outside, knowing that what awaits them is not just Earth, but their future, together.

So, we should have a vision in our life and should love our work that we'll do it in a right way, be ready to accept obstacles by not losing hope, when we use to see Veggoes rivalry with Aayun, harming others won't yield anything, so 'live and let live.' And live like a world is one.